JACKSON ALONE

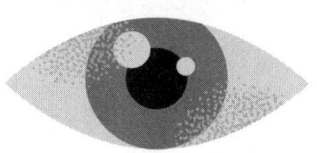

JACKSON ALONE

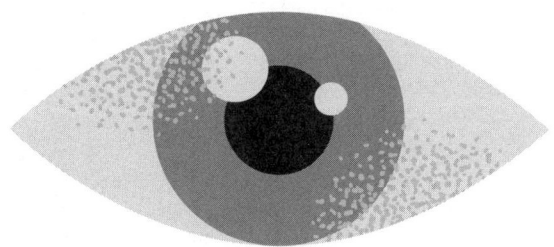

JOSE ANDO

TRANSLATED FROM THE JAPANESE BY KALAU ALMONY

First published in English in 2026 by
Soho Press
227 W 17th Street
New York, NY 10011
www.sohopress.com

First published in Japanese under the title ジャクソンひとり.
Copyright © 2022 by Jose Ando.
English translation copyright © 2026 by Kalau Almony.
All rights reserved.

Original Japanese edition published by KAWADE SHOBO SHINSHA Ltd. Publishers.
This English edition is published by arrangement with KAWADE SHOBO
SHINSHA Ltd. Publishers, Tokyo, in care of The English Agency (Japan) Ltd.
and New River Literary Ltd.

All rights reserved.

Library of Congress Cataloging-in-Publication Data

Names: Ando, Jose, 1994- author | Almony, Kalau translator
Title: Jackson alone / Jose Ando ; translated from the Japanese by Kalau Almony.
Other titles: Jakuson hitori. English
Description: New York, NY : Soho Crime, 2026.
Identifiers: LCCN 2025031641
ISBN 978-1-64129-636-6
eISBN 978-1-64129-637-3

Subjects: LCSH: Gay men—Japan—Fiction | Multiracial people—Japan—Fiction
| Corporate culture—Japan—Fiction | LCGFT: Detective and mystery fiction |
Queer fiction | Novels
Classification: LCC PL878.5.N46 J3513 2026 |
DDC 895.63/6—dc23/eng/20250714
LC record available at https://lccn.loc.gov/2025031641

Interior design by Janine Agro

Printed in the United States of America

10 9 8 7 6 5 4 3 2 1

EU Responsible Person (for authorities only)
eucomply OÜ
Pärnu mnt 139b-14
11317 Tallinn, Estonia
hello@eucompliancepartner.com
www.eucompliancepartner.com

JACKSON ALONE

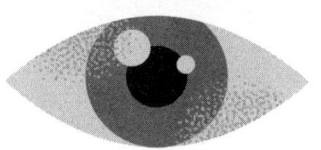

1.

The cocoa skin, the devilish eyes, too big and too bright, the limbs like a panther's. Jackson knew the moment he saw the video that the man tied to the bed was him. He didn't remember it, and he knew there were tons of people in this world who looked like him. But this was Japan, and here in Japan it was Jackson alone who looked like that and was treated this way.

THAT MORNING THE temperature had suddenly dropped, and since it felt like fall, Jackson pulled on a long-sleeve T-shirt before biking to work. The shirt was from a brand he didn't recognize, but he was almost certain his company dress code said he could wear whatever he wanted so long as it wasn't from a rival sportswear line.

On a spacious plot of reclaimed land sat two corporate-looking buildings: an office tower that loomed over the entire area and another, smaller building that looked like the first building's child. That smaller building—the staff fitness center of Athletius Japan's headquarters—was where Jackson worked. He spent all day in there, giving massages.

His schedule was packed that morning. The company basketball team's offseason had just ended in August and the players were now back in full swing. His first appointment was with the team's forward, a man called Zen. For sixty minutes, Jackson tore into Zen's muscle fibers, shocked by just how quickly they recovered from his touch. All Jackson had to do was run his fingers down Zen's back two or three times and his muscles would go from being shrunk stiff with disuse to sucking up blood and swelling with each beat of Zen's heart.

At a certain point during the session, Zen asked Jackson, "What did you wanna be when you were a teenager?"

"I really just wanted to party," Jackson said.

"Did you ever think of becoming an athlete?"

"No, never."

"Why not?"

"Because I found out about partying."

"Too bad. I bet you'd've been good . . ."

No, you're way more built for this than I am. Jackson

JACKSON ALONE

thought this but didn't say it aloud, just continued to knead his fingers into Zen's muscles.

And the conversation ends yet again, Zen thought. It always stops when we get to Jackson's turn, doesn't it? He's unreadable. That was the impression Jackson left on Zen. What did Zen know about Jackson? He was half Japanese and half some kind of African. He used to run track. He'd modeled. He might be gay. All this Zen had heard not from Jackson himself but secondhand—from the rumors his teammates passed around.

Maybe Jackson could've been a professional athlete, Zen thought. Or a professional model. Or at least worked at a more gay-friendly business. It was strange that he was here of all places, at the Athletius fitness center, massaging people. The fitness center staff were not technically employees of Athletius, and Zen and the other athletes used the facilities only for a small part of the year, so presumably Jackson mostly worked on the full-time office staff. They probably complained to Jackson about routine aches and pains, ones that were impossible to tell apart from the normal processes of aging, then just returned to their desk jobs. His days must've consisted of that and just that, over and over again.

JOSE ANDO

There were people who talked, who said Jackson had become a massage therapist only because he was gay and just wanted an excuse to touch men, but Zen knew that wasn't right. He could feel the restraint in Jackson's hands as they made their way down his back. Zen occasionally slept with men, too, but he planned to marry a girl and raise children one day. To Zen, sex with men was the same as S&M or threesomes. It was just another category of porn. He never had a problem finding someone to sleep with and wasn't really looking for a special someone at the moment.

They never did get into anything personal, but since neither of them was "pure" Japanese, they still found plenty to talk about. After the session, they added each other on LINE and parted ways. For the rest of the morning, Jackson gave massages and Zen joined team meetings. At noon, they saw each other again at the food court.

It was packed. Jackson ordered chicken breast and grain tacos with 25 g of protein and soup, then hurried to grab an open seat by the window. The fitness center staff all wore Athletius gear, so everyone looked like some sort of athlete, but the real athletes could be easily identified by their sense of superiority. They

JACKSON ALONE

held court in the center of the cafeteria, their table so messy it looked like they'd been there for hours. That was where Jackson spotted Zen again. Their glances were out of sync, though, so whenever Zen looked at Jackson, Jackson was turned away. This only reaffirmed Zen's impression of Jackson: He really was unreadable.

By lunchtime the clouds had cleared, and yesterday's full-blown summer heat had returned. Jackson took off his long-sleeve shirt and changed into his Athletius attire before he began crunching on his tacos. The food dried out his mouth. He downed each bite with soup, and, after clearing his plate in less than ten minutes, he changed the song playing on his AirPods. Suddenly he remembered the feeling of Zen's back. Though hours had passed, the sensation came alive in his fingers again and felt so real.

Zen didn't see Jackson get up from the table because he was too distracted by his teammates' chattering. They were having a field day, one-upping each other with crude gross-out stories. This girl once barfed up an expensive risotto dinner on someone's bed on their first date and it looked exactly the same as when it was on her plate . . . A former classmate's mom DM'ed someone

JOSE ANDO

a nude . . . And so on, until the topic turned to Zen's profile pic on a dating app. It was a photo of him on a mountain with—the team captain sneered—an incredibly unimpressive view behind him.

"Do you understand what this photo is saying about you?" The captain spoke gleefully, bringing his face close to Zen's phone and prodding at it. "Girls will judge your taste, man! Look at this place. Would any girl want you to take her there?"

He spoke like a talk show host would to his studio audience, explaining something everyone should already know. His lackeys chortled. Zen grew embarrassed but joined his team in laughter, all the while imagining what everyone else in the cafeteria must've thought of them. Probably that they were boring as hell.

The other team members got in on the action, adding their own commentary: *Yeah, it's a lame photo, Zen. And what's with your eyes? They're half closed . . . Why are you giving a thumbs-up? Oof, yeah, this is no good. Let's take a new one for you. According to research from some American university, you get more matches if you're holding a drink. They say if you have friends in the picture, the number of girls who think you're trustworthy increases*

JACKSON ALONE

by twenty percent. Don't worry, I'll get in the picture with you. Don't show my face, though; it should just be yours.

The captain lifted his phone and readied the camera.

"All right, don't say cheese."

When the shot was in focus, the camera picked up something behind Zen.

Thrown over the back of an empty chair was a lone shirt. In the seemingly random black-and-white pattern on its back, one could just make out a faint square. Blink and the square would dissolve back into the pattern.

What is that? The phone's reading something in the pattern on that shirt. It just looks like some streetwear design. Who was sitting there? Oh, it was Jackson. Huh . . . Look at the shirt. Fancy. Is it? That depends on what the link's to, no? It's probably just the brand's Insta or something. Check it out.

Still posing for the photo with a cup of coffee in his hand, Zen waited for this whole thing to end. The captain stared at his phone screen, not saying a word. The teammates on either side of him leaned their heads in close.

Is this a promo video? It's a little excessive for that. Yeah . . . excessive. It's kinda gay.

They laughed it off awkwardly, waiting for the next scene to play, but the video didn't cut away from the man tied to a bed.

Who's making money off this super gay branding? If this kind of thing actually sold product, our company would be all over it. I bet whoever thought this up must be real proud of themself. Wait a minute. This guy in the video . . . Is that Jackson?

At Jackson's name, Zen stood up from his chair automatically. Then he spoke, maintaining perfect calm: "Apparently he was a model before he worked here. I bet it's for some brand he used to work for."

Those who'd seen the video stared hard at Zen like some sort of alien life-form had taken his place.

"This?" The captain set the smartphone down in the middle of the table, and the team members resumed their deliberations.

Oh, he was that kind of model? Modeling? This isn't

JACKSON ALONE

modeling. We've got another name for this kind of work. Work? More like fun. Fun? You gotta be real sick to find this fun. What kind of joke is this? Why would he wear something like that to work? Maybe it's also part of some sex game? Should we report this? Is it sexual harassment? HR would faint if they saw this.

An emotional consensus ran through the team like an electric charge.

The fitness center staff around them had grown somewhat numb to the team's ruckus. A lone dispatch worker focused on his meal, despite the distinctive squeak of the athletes' shoes against the cafeteria floor giving him goose bumps. A pair of retail employees from the Athletius shop continued scrolling on their phones, paying them no mind. The head of sales, who'd brought some underlings with him to lunch, raised the volume of his voice so he didn't get drowned out. The underlings nodded along exaggeratedly to show him that it was okay, that they were still listening, but everyone, from the fragments that they'd picked up, thought the same thing: Obnoxious as these guys are, maybe they're on to something interesting this time.

The team noticed that they'd started to draw the

JOSE ANDO

attention of everyone around them, and that just got them more worked up.

What's with the Immortan Joe mask? Yeah, look, there's a tube coming out of it. And it's connected to his ass. I know what this is, it's a kind of BDSM thing, it's called "manhowling." That's not a tube, it's a cord. The thing in his mouth is a mic and there's a speaker in his ass. If he makes any noise, it'll play inside him and his whole body'll work like a speaker, then he'll make even more noise because of the pain. That repeats and it turns into hardcore feedback. It's super dangerous. What the fuck. Apparently it's super popular now. Popular where? Overseas. That sounds dangerous. Yeah, it's probably dangerous. I mean, it looks like it hurts pretty bad. Fuck. Look at how twisted up his abs are. It's like he's got an alien growing in there. Damn it, this is too good. When I think about how someone somewhere seriously thought up this kind of thing, it's just too funny. I gotta respect it. I could never come up with this . . . let alone try it? Either his head's not on straight or he's got the body of a beast. This pisses me off. I mean, let's say he's doing this for fun. That means this guy's hiding who he really is and touching our bodies every day. With that smug fucking face. I can put up with a normal homo, but this is freak territory.

JACKSON ALONE

Zen's eyes shot to the exit. He could sense that he wouldn't alter his demeanor even if Jackson returned. And then it hit him. That feeling he had about Jackson, his unreadability, it might've been a sort of warning.

Will you AirDrop me the vid? Scan it yourself. No way. I might get hacked. Fine, I'm sending it to you, and you, and you. Oh, shit. I sent it to the wrong person. Oh well. Careful what you click on.

Several phones vibrated, and soon almost everyone in the food court had watched the video.

What is this? Revenge porn? No, apparently he's into it. Apparently this was his old job. A body shouldn't move that way. Is he going to die? Isn't this dangerous? It can't be that dangerous. I mean, if he wasn't fine, how could he . . .

Jackson took bigger strides than anyone else on staff, so by the time anyone noticed him in the doorway, he was already in the middle of the food court. Those who'd been watching the video at that moment all rushed to mute their phones, but Jackson's ears picked up the sound just before it vanished. A sound like a man's scream buried under static—no, more like a man's scream distorted into static. When it stopped, the food court fell silent, and Jackson raised his eyebrows. He hurried to his table by the window and picked up his tray, the food wrappers, and his long-sleeve shirt.

The team captain gave Jackson a snide look. "Thanks for everything you do for us," he said. "The team is grateful. Your massages are always *so* thorough. Yeah, they're very thorough. In fact, everyone says they're too thorough. We can really tell you love what you do."

Jackson smirked in response, then made for the exit.

"In exchange for your hard work, let me give you some advice," the captain called out to Jackson before he reached the door. "You shouldn't wear that shirt to work."

There was always someone from apparel out on patrol, inspecting everyone's work clothes. At first, Jackson assumed the captain meant his shirt had been spotted by one of them.

"Can I see it?" the captain said, gesturing as though he were summoning the shirt toward him with his finger. Jackson tossed it over to him, and as it flew through the air, Jackson's name tag, pinned on the shirt's right side, glinted in the sunlight.

The captain caught it. He spread the shirt flat on the table, turned it over, and, acting as though he were doing

JACKSON ALONE

some sort of sleight of hand, scanned the pattern with his phone. He snuck several looks at Jackson, who was approaching nervously. The captain couldn't wait for the moment when Jackson's smug mask was ripped clean off.

And then Jackson saw the video. His flesh captured on camera who knows when, his decision today to wear that shirt, the captain's spitefulness, someone's plot to ruin him—it was frightening to see all those pieces click perfectly into place.

"Sorry," he said. "But that's not me."

The captain didn't like that Jackson was lying straight to his face, but he continued playing the nice guy. "Come on," he said. "It has to be. I mean, it's your shirt, right?"

"I didn't buy it. Someone sent it to me."

"Who?"

"I don't know," Jackson said. "I used to model. Tons of clothes just show up at my house. And even if I knew, why would I have to tell you?"

"I mean, you realize this is basically public indecency? At least that's how I see it."

"This looks to me like revenge porn," Jackson said.

"If it is, you're being real calm about it."

"Am I supposed to be visibly upset?"

JOSE ANDO

"Right, right. My bad. Our place of work is now unsafe because we had to watch you get off, but you say *you're* the victim and you have no intention of proving that to us, so we just have to shut up and deal?"

"More or less, yes." Jackson let out a snort of laughter. "But that isn't me in the video. It's someone else. Like I already said."

The fitness center staff watched this exchange from the sidelines. Some of them, too, were convinced that it was Jackson in the video. They caught themselves looking him up and down, imagining the same junk in the video hanging between Jackson's legs. Others believed Jackson. Given the speed of his responses, he must be telling the truth, they thought. Which would mean that something that looked *very similar* to the junk in the video was hanging between Jackson's legs. They wound up looking at Jackson no differently than the first group.

Jackson returned the glances of both groups by reflex, and even though there was no particular animus behind it, there was a glimmer in his gaze as he looked back, and they all quickly turned away from it. Their eyes scattered like fish struck by a sudden beam of light.

At least this guy will say it to my face, Jackson thought,

JACKSON ALONE

looking to the captain again. At least I can count on that.

"Why did you assume this was me, anyway?"

"I mean, it looks like you." The captain's response got a laugh.

"What about him looks like me?" Jackson said.

"The . . . way he looks."

"The way he looks. Can you be more specific? Which parts *exactly* look like me?"

Given the setting, there was nothing the captain could say. *Black, skin, face, hair, only you, race, this kind of person, this type.* As the captain rolled around the options in the back of his throat, he noticed Jackson's cheeks gradually rise into a grin.

"Let me ask again. What made you decide this was me?"

"Right. Got it. I see how it is. I'm sorry. I was wrong. Let's just end this."

"What? So you're the ref now, too?"

THE BELL RANG for the end of lunch. Jackson was meant to have a one o'clock appointment, but when he returned to the massage room, no one was there. He checked his schedule on the computer and found that the appointment had been canceled. While he'd vaguely expected this, he still felt a sudden pang in his stomach. As he stared at the monitor, five more cancellation notifications appeared in a row and suddenly all his appointments for the day were gone. He changed the calendar view to see his schedule for the week and watched as appointment after appointment disappeared. The moment he thought he was done for, though, his schedule began to fill with new requests, and in less than half an hour, about 70 percent of his appointments had been refilled. All names he'd never seen before. The sight of these unexpected supporters moved Jackson. He was grateful not to have been reduced to zero sessions, but he also knew these new clients weren't actually going to fix anything.

Jackson tapped his full lips with two fingers, sucked a breath in, then exhaled imaginary smoke. No one was there, and even Jackson had no idea who he was playing it cool for. He figured no one would come in for a while, so he spread out the shirt that he'd crumpled into a ball and stuffed between his thighs.

It was true that as a model he'd received a ton of free clothes. A few months after ending his contract with

JACKSON ALONE

Mannequin Management and before starting subcontract work at Athletius, he'd found a package sticking out of his mailbox. He clawed open the wrapping and felt the roughness of 100 percent cotton. A spark of joy ran through him when he saw the design, a glitched-out black-and-white checkerboard, and he added the shirt to his clothing rack. The summer heat had been unending, though, so today had been his first time wearing it.

It was strange. Jackson hadn't noticed anything off about the shirt. But now that he knew about the trick in the shirt's pattern, he couldn't see anything else. He scanned it with his phone and, sure enough, the camera caught the QR code.

Jackson saw his skin fill the glowing screen of his phone. He winced for a second but found himself surprisingly capable of remaining calm as he watched. He had absolutely no memory of this. And that was why, strangely enough, he could watch the video as if through someone else's eyes and have the irresponsible reaction he did: Below the desk, blood began to rush to his crotch. The ideal response of a member of a collective and the actual feelings of an individual never perfectly coincide. By Jackson's calculations, if he took his arousal out of the equation, then his reaction would just about equal that of a normal viewer.

The man in the video hadn't done anything wrong, Jackson concluded. There was no reason for him to feel embarrassed. *He's only human, after all. But I do feel bad for him. But also, in a way, he makes for an interesting character.* Jackson took note of what he was feeling in that moment and decided to hang on to his reaction as a sort of good-luck charm.

In the final scene of the video, an arm reached in from off-screen. It was a man's arm, the kind you could see anywhere in Japan. The motion it made was less like jerking off and more like ramming its fist into the stomach of the man on the bed. It made him come. Then the video ended.

Jackson didn't have to replay the video to be certain what hotel it was. He'd been there often enough to identify the carpeting, which was patterned with a map of the world. It was next to the nature park in the middle of the city, almost exactly halfway between Athletius's plot of reclaimed land and Jackson's house. Hotel Sagitari.

That evening, after his last client had left, Jackson

JACKSON ALONE

locked the massage room and biked to the hotel. On his way, he was stopped and questioned by the police. In the bluish evening light, the officer told Jackson to turn on his lights, then checked the registry to make sure Jackson hadn't stolen the bike. In the few minutes he was stopped, Jackson began to sweat and his Athletius shirt stuck to his skin. Once the officer let him go and he was sure no one was around, he changed into the long-sleeve shirt he'd hidden in his bag. With his backpack on, no one could see the pattern on his back.

"DO YOU SAVE security camera footage?"

The man at the hotel front desk hesitated to answer Jackson's question. Jackson had expected they would refuse to show him the security footage, so he leaned his weight on the counter and, in a soft voice, broke into an explanation.

"I've stayed here before, and I had a bit of trouble," he said. "I'm planning to file a report with the police. I'm just worried I don't have enough evidence."

Jackson's plan was to play the victim of an imaginary

crime, but he realized everything he was saying was, in fact, the truth. When he understood this, the blood began to rush just below his skin. Just as it had so many times that afternoon.

"When was it that you stayed with us?" The man sounded suspicious.

"About a year ago."

"One year?" The man looked down at the monitor and after a pause, repeated, "One year. I see." He asked for Jackson's name to search their records. Sensing that they either did not have the footage or that getting it would require considerable negotiation, Jackson offered a smile, said thank you, and left the hotel without giving his name. He went back to the park, took off the shirt in a public bathroom near the lake, and changed back into his Athletius shirt.

AT WORK THE next day, Jackson's eleven o'clock had a sore back. To evaluate the man's muscle stiffness, Jackson had him lie on his side as Jackson pressed down on his lower back. The man grunted.

"Nobody else thinks this hurts?" he said.

JACKSON ALONE

"No, everyone says it hurts a lot," Jackson replied.

"I bet. It hurts like a motherfucker."

"Yeah, it hurts so bad I literally jump whenever someone does it to me."

"Even though you do it to other people?"

"Some of us have bodies that can't help but overreact, you know?"

"Yeah, you're right. Some bodies are like that." The man emphasized the word *bodies*, and laughed.

"Yeah, that's how my body is," Jackson said.

The man's pupils darted to the corners of his eyes to catch a glimpse of Jackson's face. Jackson felt those eyes relaying their pity to him. *It's not your fault*, they seemed to say. *You were assaulted by someone.* Ah, I see, thought Jackson. In this man's mind, I'm a victim. A fever raced through his body followed by a rapid chill. It was as if a wound that had never existed had suddenly reopened deep inside him. His body seemed to recall the inflammation from having the silver speaker inserted into him, the metal crosshatch tearing him up. Maybe he did remember what was in that video. The massage room filled with a sense of gloom, and Jackson spent the remaining forty-six minutes playing a certain version of himself: Jackson the Pitiful.

JOSE ANDO

His one o'clock appointment was with a guy Jackson recognized from the cafeteria yesterday. With him in the room, everything changed, and Jackson wound up taking on a new role: Jackson the Scandalous.

The client was amazed to see there was a TV in the room that could connect to streaming services. Jackson handed him the remote and watched as he flipped to a reality show called *Lies and Pies*. Jackson had never heard of it before. The thumbnail showed a Black man and a white woman facing each other on what looked like a quintessential American talk show set. The pair were clearly not professional TV hosts or actors. The woman was wearing a white T-shirt with fabric so worn it was nearly sheer, and the man an overly tight floral-print dress shirt. The description below the thumbnail read: *Ordinary people take the stage in this reality show meets talk show. Contestants interview each other and try to expose their opponent's faults for a cash prize.*

The concept: In front of a packed live studio audience, one contestant interviews the other, then at the end the audience votes and decides who they want to stay. The winner moves on to the next battle; the loser gets pied in the face. In principle, contestants have to

JACKSON ALONE

answer all questions; they can lie, but they have to keep in mind that lying too much could lead to losing audience votes. If they decide not to answer a question, they have to take a shot.

When his client switched the TV from *Lies and Pies* to YouTube, Jackson figured he'd gotten bored of the show, but instead a gossip channel devoted to *Lies and Pies* filled the screen. Jackson and the client were drawn into the story of how one of the recent finalists regularly attended "drug parties."

"Everyone fucks up," Jackson's client said, looking up at him. There was no bite to his comment; it seemed he was genuinely offering support to Jackson. If I were him and he were me, I'd probably take the same stance, Jackson thought. I'd be a little bit more sensitive about it, though. Jackson wrinkled up his wide nose and smiled like Jackson the Scandalous would. His client quickly averted his eyes. Jackson's body was again struck by sudden fever before going cold again.

Everyone on staff who came for a massage that day was quick to avoid Jackson's gaze. After experiencing this a few times, Jackson was overcome by a desire to hold those evasive eyes in place with his fingers. He

JOSE ANDO

imagined it then: With the same force he used to trace out the knots in their muscles, he would capture the whites of their eyes and then stick needles clean into the pupils. This fantasy calmed his fit of anger.

JACKSON TOLD HIMSELF that today would be the day he'd finally go to the police, but somehow he found himself drawn to the park near Hotel Sagitari instead. He could see the hotel's lights shining through the park's trees. Near the darkest hedge gathered an oddly large number of shadows. Jackson knew the shadows were men. Hiding behind trees, mounting benches, forming circles in the shrubbery, in every imaginable place, there were men touching one another. When the lights of his bike pierced the darkness, the men, sensing danger, scattered. And when they realized that the light did not belong to someone who held authority over them, their sense of danger faded and they flocked together again. One after another, they fled from the light of Jackson's bicycle, then flowed back into place in the darkness behind him. Just like fish, they scattered when a light hit them. It's just like them, Jackson thought, remembering

JACKSON ALONE

all the eyes in the food court. Just piloting his bicycle absentmindedly, he could make these men respond in such funny ways.

These night safaris had become a routine of Jackson's. He started taking the route through the park on the way home every day. Sometimes he would take multiple laps before heading home. One night, after he'd exhausted his enjoyment from his usual methods, he tried something else. He turned off his bicycle light and pedaled forward to the edge of a bunch of shrubbery—slowly, so the chain wouldn't make noise as it spun. When he got there, he suddenly flipped the switch on, revealing men tangled together in the most intricate of poses and sending the whole mass of them bursting apart all at once. The hopeless faces, the wrinkles of shirts pulled over heads, were seared into Jackson's retinas as the sound of footsteps on the grass faded into the distance.

THE FOLLOWING DAY, Jackson filed his report at the police station.

Before he went in, he'd searched "revenge porn victim" online. While his anger built each time he saw text assuming the victim to be a woman—images of a beautiful blond woman, her head in her hands, or Shōwa-style illustrations with lines like *I'll show everyone your dirty pictures!*—he got the basic idea of how to file a report, and also confirmed that this probably would not lead to any resolution.

The officer who took the report stared at Jackson impassively. Jackson swallowed. The man laid his right hand flat on his head and brought it forward in a straight line in Jackson's direction.

"How tall are you?" he asked quietly.

"What?"

"Your height."

"About 189 centimeters."

The man laughed in the back of his throat and leaned back exaggeratedly as if blown away by the information.

"I'm sorry. You're so tall, I was surprised."

"Really? I've been standing right in front of you for about thirty minutes."

Jackson biked through the park again on his way home. He pedaled with his lights off. The second he felt his bike dig into someone's flesh, he slammed on his brakes. His bike came to a clean stop, but the man

JACKSON ALONE

went flying. This was the third man he'd hit in the park. Onlookers froze and tried to get a good look at him, but Jackson blinded them by flipping his light to strobe mode. Nobody had seen his face.

EVEN AFTER JACKSON had sped off on his bike, the man he'd hit remained crouched where he'd landed. When someone raced over to him, the man let out a faint laugh and ran away. He was out of breath. On the palms of his hands were indentations in the shapes of pebbles and little dribbles of blood, but they didn't hurt all that much. They'd heal soon enough. The bottom of his polo shirt was stained with a tire mark. He couldn't wipe it off with his hand, but he was sure that it would come out in the wash, and that made him feel better. A voice, half laughing, saying *We thought you'd like this, Toshi-san,* played back in his mind. A long time ago, back when he'd quit his job in university admin, a flamboyant kid he'd barely known had chosen the shirt as a leaving present for him, his goodbye gift from the entire office staff. Whenever he imagined the true intention behind that kid choosing such a gay-looking shirt for him even though he had never come out to anyone at the office, Toshi still felt his face grow warm with embarrassment.

He passed through the park gate and rejoined the flow of cars and pedestrians. There was no hint of him or the other men roaming the darkness; instead, things seemed to be moving as they should be. In the distance, young people were skateboarding on an overpass, and even that looked correct. As Toshi passed a bike going in the opposite direction right next to the guardrail, the face of the cyclist came into focus under the orange glow of the streetlights. Toshi's heart began to race.

He was overcome by a powerful sense of déjà vu as he watched the man recede into the distance. Skin so dark he might've been Black, eyes like a doll's, long limbs like a model's. He looked exactly like this guy he knew, this guy named Jerin.

2.

Jerin was a part-time doorboy for Lamero, a luxury fashion brand with a shop on the first floor of the building where Toshi worked security. Given the tenuousness of their connection, it would've been risky for Toshi to try to pick up Jerin at work. If he messed it up, that would be the end of it—he would have no second chance. But one day, he discovered a weapon that would guarantee he secured his prey: Jerin's long-sleeve T-shirt.

The monitor in the security room was divided into sixteen sections, and Toshi could check the hallways and the exits of the different departments at any time. One day after closing, Jerin was leaning on the elevator wall, which was polished to a mirrorlike shine. Whenever Jerin was on-screen, Toshi automatically started recording with his phone. He wasn't sure when this had become a habit of his. When he saw something that excited him, he wanted to touch it. If he couldn't, his brain registered that as a sort of loss, and he'd begin filming in secret to compensate for the perceived privation. So Toshi pointed his phone at Jerin on the elevator.

If Toshi were to believe what he saw in that video, Jerin would be overjoyed to be manhandled by him! And if Jerin turned him down, he could just blackmail him with the video. Now that he had this flawless plan, Toshi began behaving like a totally different person, one with absolute confidence.

It started with a meaningless conversation in the bathroom. To Jerin, Toshi was just some older guy. Jerin didn't recognize him, but he had a security badge on his jacket. He could also see that this man's eyes, reflected in the mirror, were stuck on him—excessively so, Jerin felt. Toshi made himself more and more direct, as if trying to stay one step ahead of the naughty thoughts beginning to blossom in Jerin's mind.

Since coming to Japan, Jerin had found it difficult to be submissive. In his dirty talk with other men, there would inevitably be something, some word he couldn't accept, that would snap him out of it. They were supposed to be saying naughty things for him, but the men would always wind up saying something racist. *Sorry. I'm sure you didn't mean anything bad by it, but please don't say that*, Jerin would say patiently, and it would turn his partners weak with guilt.

So Jerin did feel a genuine desire for a quiet man like Toshi to pursue him. They went to a hotel, and there, too, Jerin didn't turn down a single one of Toshi's demands.

"What was it like to hear your own voice in your ass?" Toshi asked, unable to help himself. He was speaking not to Jerin but into Jerin's anus.

"You don't have to lie. You might wear a fancy suit to Lomero, but you probably get paid less than me. I don't have any reason to blackmail you. Walking around with a video of your kinks on your back . . . Did your master order you to do that or something? Or is it some kind of fad?" Toshi continued to speak into the gap between Jerin's legs, which were spread wide, and Jerin heard but did not register Toshi's words. He was looking at the phone on his stomach.

JOSE ANDO

In the video, Jerin got in the elevator and leaned on the wall near the door.

"Here," Toshi said, reaching for the phone. He took a screenshot of the scene, then opened the photo in a QR code reader.

Text immediately appeared on the top of the screen. Jerin tapped the link with his unbound left hand, and up popped a video of someone who looked just like him tied to a bed.

Jerin and the guy in the video: To Jerin it was obvious that the man was someone else, but, he realized, Toshi couldn't tell the two apart.

In the country where Jerin was born, there were countless men who looked like him and the guy in the video. Was that the only reason he could notice the slight differences between them? Was it like how he, who'd just come to Japan, couldn't tell the difference between the kanji 二 and katakana ニ?

JACKSON ALONE

The Japanese necessary to explain the situation escaped Jerin, so he just shook his head silently.

Toshi's come-on in the bathroom hadn't been fate or anything so meaningful—it had been a calculated trap. Everything was that shirt's fault. And there, for the first time, Jerin heard the things Toshi was saying as the threat they were. Like a sleight of hand after the trick has been revealed, Toshi's appeal began to fade.

There was no way Jerin could solve this by himself. He fretted over the situation late into the night until he finally decided to seek help. The person most likely to be the man in the video, as far as he knew, was a man named Ibuki.

IBUKI WAS A mixed-race Black Japanese man who uploaded his own porno videos on a pay-per-view fan site. For someone based in Japan, he had many followers overseas. Jerin had also known about Ibuki before coming to Japan.

If Jerin paid for the $20.01 option, he could message Ibuki directly. Jerin signed up and messaged his request.

JOSE ANDO

Hi Ibuki, konnichiwa. I'm sorry, but I have something not very happy to ask about even though this is my first DM.

He attached a photo of the shirt, then hurried to copy and paste the message he'd drafted ahead of time.

This shirt I got at a club has a QR code on it. I don't know who I got it from. I wore it without realizing anything. Now someone's blackmailing me

He attached a screenshot from the video.

Is this you in this video? he messaged. He worried about what he'd do if Ibuki said it wasn't him, so he frantically deleted that last message before Ibuki could read it. Everything was too complicated. Jerin was perplexed by the whole situation, so how could he know what to say to Ibuki?

It's me in the video, Jerin wrote instead, but I don't know what to do. I know it's weird for me to come to you about this, but there's no one else. What would you do if it was you?

This was a lie, but it seemed like an easier approach. Jerin didn't have the mental energy to think things through more. He hit Send.

As Ibuki went through all the messages he'd received that day, responding with a template he tweaked slightly for each, his eyes stopped on Jerin's icon. His photo

JACKSON ALONE

reminded Ibuki of a younger version of himself, and he immediately felt a sort of attachment to him. When he read Jerin's message, that attachment transformed into a sense of responsibility, a feeling that he had to help him somehow.

Thanks for the message, Ibuki wrote. **That's so stressful! I'm really freaking out lol,** Jerin responded.

For about a minute after the Read mark appeared on the message, there was no reply. Jerin had about given up. But just slightly faster than he could finish typing **I'm sorry to bother you. Don't worry about it,** there came another message from Ibuki.

Should we try saying it's me?

Ibuki had just one question he needed answered before uploading this video to his own paid channel: Was that man in the video really Jerin? After they'd said hi and reintroduced themselves over a video call, Ibuki asked him point-blank, but Jerin just nodded.

"Okay," Ibuki said. "I can't really put into words why, but you and the person in the video look a little different to me. But I guess that's a trick of the camera."

Ibuki shrugged and explained the risks of uploading someone else's video. If he were to violate someone else's portrait rights, his account would be frozen and he wouldn't be able to transfer any of the profits he'd made into his bank account. In order to upload the video, he'd need written confirmation that Jerin was the person appearing there.

"I'm going to upload it. Okay?" Ibuki said.

But when pressed, Jerin showed a little hesitation. "You sure?"

Ibuki sensed immediately the possibility that Jerin was lying but said, "As long as you don't say anything about it," and winked to the camera. He had Jerin send him a photo of his passport and a signed PDF of his agreement to appear on Ibuki's page.

Then Ibuki released the video to his platform. He also uploaded a short preview clip to Twitter. Jerin saved the post and reclaimed his life. Even if Toshi came on to him again, now he could snub him with confidence.

Several days later, however, Ibuki took the video down from all his platforms. His friend X had messaged him in protest.

That's not you in your new post, is it? I don't want to hear your lies. Just delete it immediately.

This was Ibuki's first message from X in a long time.

JACKSON ALONE

The texts he sent sounded aggressive, but when Ibuki video called him, X smiled big and said, "Hey! Long time," with his usual soft and breathy voice. After Ibuki finished explaining the situation, X responded, "Oh, I see," and bared his teeth again. His facial expression took the shape of a smile, but Ibuki knew it was an intimidation tactic. It was like when they went drinking. The more customers or staff he didn't like intruded on their space, the more X smiled. The key to tell that it was his threatening smile was to look at his jaw: He clenched his back teeth far more tightly than was normal for a carefree grin, so tightly that his jaw pulsed with a regular rhythm as though there were a small heart buried in it.

X liked to tell funny stories about his failures. Like how back in college he had basically been forced by one of his friends to start a comedy duo, or the story he told the first time they met, about how an upperclassman had invited him to go drinking three-on-three with rich older women he'd met in Roppongi and X was so bad at acting straight that they ditched him at the second club they went to. But when Ibuki had repeated that story to others and some guy made a crack at him, saying, "I'd be scared to go out drinking with you, too," X turned to him with that threatening smile.

In other words, to Ibuki, X was the type of person who enjoyed making people laugh but hated being laughed at. The fact that this video situation involved neither form of laughter made Ibuki consider the possibility that the person in the video was in fact X.

He looks truly pissed, Ibuki thought. Ibuki was over this whole thing, but he racked his brain and proposed that the three of them—Ibuki, X, and Jerin—get together and talk it out. X's suspicion hadn't faltered, but he agreed to the meeting on a few conditions. There couldn't be anyone else there. It had to be in a hotel room, which Ibuki would pay for with the money he'd made from that video. And whatever it took, even if it involved tricking him into it, Ibuki would bring Jerin.

Ibuki agreed to everything. He would've done anything to get X to drop it.

The three of them agreed to meet that Friday night at Hotel Sagitari. Jerin arrived at the front of the hotel and waited, but then Ibuki messaged him requesting that he wait at the back entrance where there was no reception

JACKSON ALONE

desk, so he rushed up the stone stairs to the other side of the hotel. Jerin had always wanted to meet Ibuki, and soon he would. He danced up the steps. As he climbed higher, the plants along the sides of the stairs grew thicker. His hand slid up along the cold handrail, and it made a rustling sound as it brushed against leaves and branches. From the top of the steps, he could see that the trees belonged to a park. The night sky was framed in green. He realized that Hotel Sagitari protruded into that park.

Following the path, he soon found the back entrance to the hotel. Right beside it, he saw someone on a bike looking away from him and slapped his hand on their back, just above the ass.

Jackson was shocked to be suddenly touched and couldn't catch what the guy was saying in English. Though he missed what the man had said, Jackson still placed his own hand on top of the one on his back. He couldn't tell whether this guy had mistaken him for a friend or wanted to become his friend, or maybe had mistaken him for someone he was to have sex with, or was inviting him to have sex; he seemed to be so cheerful a person that it could have been any of the above. Jackson squeezed the person's hand back, and it felt like squeezing his own anesthetized hand.

Jerin turned around and lifted the back of his sweater. His shirt underneath was covered with a black-and-white checkerboard pattern.

Jackson couldn't find the words to express his surprise.

"I'm sorry. You're the wrong person, aren't you?" Jerin said nervously.

Jackson was frozen stiff. "Maybe not," he whispered before reaching out for the shirt, showing no sign of hesitation. Sebum leaked from his forehead and glittered like tears.

"But who are you?"

"I'm Jackson."

"Nice to meet you."

"I've got one of those shirts, too."

"No way."

Ibuki and X appeared. Ibuki pushed open the glass door with the tip of his shoe. *What's this?* He froze in place. There were two men at the door, both of whom looked like Jerin. The one on the bicycle was pulling a wrinkled piece of fabric out of his backpack. The one

JACKSON ALONE

standing up reached for it as well. Together they spread open a long-sleeve shirt.

"Aren't there one too many of you?" Ibuki said as he waved, his white teeth spilling out from behind his lips.

"You didn't mention he was bringing a friend," X complained, quietly enough so only Ibuki could hear, but Ibuki, without dropping his grin, whispered back, "We don't know that he invited him. And getting mad at me won't help anything." Ibuki gestured for the two men looking worriedly at him from the dark to come along.

X decided he wouldn't greet them. With his arms crossed, he looked down and rubbed the bottom of his shoe against the ground.

Jackson couldn't process what was happening. He had thought he'd found another Jackson, then two more had appeared. The Jackson Four. He thought about making a joke—*Should we invite one more and start a band?*—but judging from the vibes, he was the uninvited guest, so he decided against it.

"Am I getting in the way of something here?" Jackson whispered to Jerin.

"Maybe it'd be better if you stayed, actually," Jerin replied with a wry smile.

Ibuki shook hands with both of them at the door. They caught up with X, who had his middle finger on the elevator button, and the four of them headed up to the room.

3.

"So, I know we all wanna talk about who's actually in that video . . ."

Ibuki threw himself ass-first onto the bed and untied his shoes. There were two single beds in the room. One bed was wrinkled from someone sitting there, and the other, which had been pristine, was now also wrinkled thanks to Ibuki.

Only Ibuki looked different from the other three, though this might not have always been true. Jerin was sure that when he'd first found Ibuki online, he had looked more like them. But Ibuki had kept getting tattoos. A few years ago, he stopped updating his channel, and when he resumed activity a year later, he had even more tattoos and had grown a beard, and his voice had gotten lower. Jerin tried to see through this Ibuki, who'd become so trendy. As he pictured the younger Ibuki, who must've still been buried somewhere within him, their gazes met. Ibuki's eyes had maintained their youth. Their inner corners opened wide and their pink membranes glittered as though lined with rhinestones.

". . . but I don't want to get into it. In a way, searching for who it really is is worse than searching for the criminal, right? And it seems like a few of us here have already claimed to be in it."

Jerin swallowed. X smiled with his eyes closed.

"*And*, if we consider the broader possibilities," Ibuki continued, "maybe it's not any of us here. Only the person in the video could really know. Digging into that sort of thing feels a bit second-rapey. It does none of us any good to snoop."

In his head, X spewed venom—Well, that's rich coming from someone just in it for the money. You've been selling that video for a minute, haven't you?—but he kept the snark to himself. He looked down and listened carefully, making sure Ibuki's roundabout start didn't steer the conversation away from what they'd privately discussed before this meeting.

An hour earlier, X and Ibuki had met to put together their own game plan. The two of them didn't discuss how to find out who was really in that video but rather

JACKSON ALONE

who should assume the role. Their thinking was, if they could all agree on one person to become the man in the video, and make sure no one else claimed to be him, then the others could act like they knew nothing about it—and that way, if anyone really grilled them, they'd have someone else's testimony as proof it wasn't them. This was the most effective way to protect all of them. Ibuki explained this to the others now.

"Is that okay with those of you just joining us today?" he asked, turning to Jackson.

Jackson saluted and answered, "Any claim I had to that video is all yours."

"Why are you acting like you're the one doing us a favor?" X shot back at Jackson, the words racing out of his mouth.

Jackson wasn't fazed by X's irritated tone. "Just now Ibuki said you wanted to protect 'all of us.' But nobody expected me here today, right?" he said. "That means you were planning this all just for Jerin. That sounds a little *too* altruistic to me. You've never even met Jerin before, and if Ibuki wanted to protect you, he could have done that without our permission. Just like he did until last week."

JOSE ANDO

"You follow my account!" Ibuki hugged himself and wiggled his body, feigning coyness.

Fake as hell! X thought as he twisted his face into an expression of disgust, then turned to Jackson with a smile and said, "Okay, so . . . Jackson-san, right? What's your point?"

"My point is, it doesn't sound like you're doing us the favor of taking on that role. It sounds like you're just trying to get us to shut up about it."

"That's fucking funny. What are you? A lawyer?"

"I'm a physical therapist."

"Wow, what a waste. You're too good a talker for that." X's words dripped with sarcasm.

"I'm glad you picked up quick," Ibuki jumped in. He clapped his hands together to change the vibe and, with his eyes, signaled to X to help instead of pick fights.

X gave an ironic shrug, and Ibuki exhaled through his nose and raised his voice a notch. "Do you watch *Lies and Pies?*" he said. "You know of it at least, right? Well, X-kun here is going to be in the Tokyo series. And it seems like they're really going to grill him over this whole shirt incident."

"That's that show where someone just had to quit?"

JACKSON ALONE

Jackson asked, recalling the YouTube video from a few days ago.

"Yeah, what was his name? X, what was it?"

"Umm . . ."

"Evelynn Dewy?" Jerin answered enthusiastically. He held his mouth in the shape of the final *ee* and tilted his head in doubt.

Ibuki and Jackson got a little worked up over Jerin's answer. *Oh, you know about it! I guess the show really is famous.* X, on the other hand, wiped the inquisitive look from his face and gave Jerin the side-eye. Then, stubbornly ignoring Jerin, he repeated, "Oh, right, Evelynn Dewy," as though he'd happened to spot the answer written somewhere on the wall.

Jerin sensed that this X guy probably knew he'd lied to Ibuki about being the person in the video. He felt awkward and decided to keep his mouth shut for a while.

Jackson acted oblivious to the tension between the two. He took out his phone and asked X, "Will you show up if I search the name X online?"

"I'm using a stage name, so probably not."

"What should I search, then?"

"*Adam*," Ibuki cut in. From his tone it was clear he was poking fun at X.

"Why 'Adam'?" Jackson asked, laughing along with Ibuki.

"I figured any name would do, so I decided to reuse my name from when I used to turn tricks."

Jackson wasn't finished with his questions. "How did the show find out about the video?"

"I wore that shirt to the audition. I had no idea what it was until some assholes from the documentary crew caught it on camera."

"Documentary crew? You mean they're making something else besides the show?"

"Yeah, there are these YouTube-exclusive behind-the-scenes videos following the contestants' auditions."

"And you wore that shirt for it?" Jackson sounded oddly giddy as he asked.

"Yep. And they took that episode down real fast," X said.

"It would make things pretty complicated if someone else posted that video, too," said Jackson.

"Yeah. And it sucks that it looks like I lied to get on the show." X glared at Jerin, then shifted his gaze away

JACKSON ALONE

when he sensed in Jerin's face that he was about to apologize.

"I took it down right away. It'll be fine," said Ibuki. He spoke softly, as if trying to put himself at ease.

"Is there a prize?" Jackson asked.

"Of course."

"Oh, so it could be your big break," Jackson prodded, his words barbed.

"It's pretty fucked up, given the situation, to see it as a break. But it is one," Ibuki said. "I say we let X act like he's the guy in the video and the rest of us pretend we know nothing." Ibuki stood up, raising both arms like he had just crossed a finish line.

"So we agree? Step one: Complete."

There was no need to discuss what step two was. They all knew: Identify the criminal.

Ibuki asked when each had gotten their shirts, and Jackson, Jerin, and X all responded at once.

Sometime before summer. Two months ago. Recently.

They heard one another's answers while giving their own, and since the other responses sounded like they might be right, too, each speaker's confidence wavered and the final inflections of their answers blurred together. Ibuki laughed, his teeth at least ten times brighter than the others'. "This isn't elementary school. We're not comparing homework answers."

They then took turns telling their own stories: Jackson's shirt arrived in his mailbox at the end of May. Jerin found his in late July—he was performing in a drag show when the shirt was thrown onstage along with a bunch of fake roses that cost 1,000 yen a piece. X found his shirt on August 21. He wasn't sure what to wear that day, and as he was pulling clothes off his shelves, he found it mixed in with his own wardrobe, looking like something he might've bought a long time ago. X could give a specific date because he'd texted one of his regular hookups and asked if he'd forgotten the shirt at his place. The four examined the message on X's phone, bringing their heads so close in proximity that you could hear their hair rubbing together, and let out sighs of relief when they realized the QR code wasn't in the picture.

So, they'd each gotten their shirts at a different time, nobody's memory of it was completely certain, and the lag between the trap being set and its discovery was far too long.

JACKSON ALONE

• • •

A WEEK LATER, all but Ibuki brought their past year of phone records to Hotel Sagitari. They transferred all the data they had to X's MacBook and scanned their paper records to send to him. X used the search function to check for any numbers that were shared between more than one of them.

X worked away silently, leaving Jackson and Jerin with nothing to do. They didn't want to look like they were just loafing, though, so they compared their chat histories on hookup apps. It was so obvious that they were just trying to look busy that they started to irritate X.

Ibuki had turned down sharing his own phone history, claiming that since he hadn't received a shirt, he didn't consider himself involved. He gave them the hotel room number, then, an hour later, joined to deliver them cookies. From the pocket of his PUMA x Maison Kitsuné collaboration sweatpants he pulled out cookies individually wrapped in clear plastic. They had a homemade look to them, not like something you'd buy from a bakery.

Ibuki plopped down onto the still-unwrinkled bed the three had for some reason avoided, and shimmied off his sweatpants. Even close up, not a single pore was visible on his thighs, and Jackson gulped, thinking to himself, These are porn-star legs. With his gold-tipped fingernails, Ibuki broke a cookie in half, placed half on his own tongue, then handed Jackson one of the whole cookies.

"Just a half of a half is probably enough to start with," Ibuki suggested. Jackson did as he was told and put a quarter of the cookie in his mouth, then handed the other quarter to Jerin, who ate it. What was left in the bag must've been half a cookie, but it had completely fallen apart and was now just a mound of crumbs. While Jerin hesitated to hand the bag of crumbs to X, who seemed uptight about such things, Ibuki took the clean half he was holding on to and put it in X's mouth. As the four chewed on their cookies, an earthy, herbal fragrance spread through their mouths.

After a while, X slammed his MacBook shut. "This is useless. I can't find anything."

His eyes were glassy but contained a hint of cheerfulness. He bugged Ibuki for more cookie, and when Ibuki said, "I'm not giving you any more," X replied, "That's why you don't have any friends," and reached for the complimentary chocolates on the table. "I've got fans,

JACKSON ALONE

so I'm fine," Ibuki shot back. The other three watched as X clumsily peeled away the golden aluminum wrapping, the chocolate looking as if it would melt from X's body heat before it was unwrapped. By the time X had finished licking his sticky fingers, the other three were entranced, their eyes fixed on him.

The carpet beneath Jackson's feet suddenly felt scratchy, and he gave it a hard look. Lemon-yellow lines crisscrossed on a faded brown background, forming a map of the world. It was the same carpet in the video, the same carpet he'd seen when he'd frequented this hotel. They must have used the same carpet in all the rooms here.

Back when Jackson had come here regularly, he'd drink whatever was offered to him by whomever he came to fool around with, and he'd frequently black out. When this happened, he would tell himself that it was a "necessary cost." His memory of the carpet, though, was vivid, and that had been his proof that he was the person in the video. But now, as he spent more time as one of four Jacksons, his sense that he was the one who'd endured it, that sense that had weighed down on him so heavily, began to melt away.

When Jackson placed his foot on one of the yellow

lines on the carpet, he thought it felt slightly different somehow. Jerin felt the same strangeness. He wondered why he could sense with his skin that there was a line there even though just the color of it was different. Maybe the dye affected the stiffness of the fibers and the skin on his foot was able to pick that up. He rubbed his sole against the carpet to check.

"Jerin, you think it's strange, too?" Jackson asked.

"Huh? Yeah."

"The way these lines feel?"

"Yeah! How'd you know?"

"That's my father's country," X said, joining in and pointing to a small island by Jackson's foot.

"That's Japan!"

"Yup."

"Mom's country is around this leg of the table."

The table was encircled by the African continent.

"I'm here and here," Ibuki said, spreading his legs wide, putting his left foot near X's and brushing his right against the tip of Jackson's.

"Isn't your dad on base? I thought he was US military," X asked disinterestedly.

"No idea what he's doing anymore. He always

JACKSON ALONE

called himself American, but obviously he's got roots somewhere else," Ibuki answered, snorting in laughter. "And anyway," he continued, tracing an arc like a compass with his left leg and pushing gently on the table with the tips of his toes, "look! The distance is the same." He spread both his arms out like a skateboarder to try and keep his balance, but he lost it and grabbed on to Jackson's hands to keep from falling. When Jackson squeezed his fingers, Ibuki squeezed back even harder, and Jackson understood what Ibuki wanted. Ibuki's hands were rough, full of cracks and veins, the hands of an older man. They made Jackson think of the father he'd never seen, the older brother he'd never had.

"What about you, Jackson?"

"Here," he said, and stuck his right foot where Ibuki's and X's feet had met. "And the other one's a mystery." He pushed his big toe hard against the carpet, and the color began to drain from it, turning pale like custard.

"So somewhere above this line?" Ibuki asked, roughly dragging his toenails across the carpet. He managed to make a clean half circle around Japan by standing up the fibers. "Hey, not bad, huh?"

JOSE ANDO

Jerin went and stood in front of X and then stuck a foot under the TV stand.

"Jerin's the only one who's different. Both his left and his right."

"But the distance between the two is probably the same," X said, taking Jerin's hands and lifting them up.

"Ha ha, you're all about distance tonight."

Jerin and X faced each other. Holding both Jerin's hands, X began to spin around with him as in a ballroom dance. The occasional applause or burst of laughter broke out in the room. Jerin dragged his toes across the carpet, tracing circles, until his leg scraped against a corner of the bed. His voice rang out. His leg was in the air, then slammed into Ibuki's. They all lost their balance and fell onto the bed.

When they closed their eyes, the previous scene played across the backs of their eyelids. Their feet were as shaky as jelly, the map of the world wobbled, and someone's legs grazed that surface. The lemon-yellow lines began to distort, like an image reflected in a puddle. The room smelled like earth, and their throats were dry. Who they were, what they were made of, where they came from, where they were, all of that stopped mattering as they fell asleep.

JACKSON ALONE

• • •

WHEN JACKSON WOKE up, the room was a total mess. Four legs were sticking out of a balled-up comforter on the other bed. He could see a foot with gold-painted toenails, and another with a bloody pinkie toe wrapped in place with tissue. Jerin and Ibuki. That would mean the person next to Jackson, still as the dead, was X. On the nightstand next to the window was a pile of monochromatic vintage clothing. All high-end brands, and black. Jackson knew they belonged to X.

Jackson got up to use the bathroom. When he finished and closed the lid of the toilet, a sports bra came down on top of it. He pictured everyone's chests and silently placed the bra next to Jerin. Jerin was still asleep, using Ibuki's arm as a pillow. The edges of the letters carved into Ibuki's arm formed a jagged arc and looked as though they were tangled up in Jerin's hair.

The table was covered by the marks of Ibuki's presence. In the middle of the night, someone had complained they were thirsty and Ibuki had offered them orange juice. Now there was the half-transparent stickiness of dried-up juice spilled from a cup. The bunch of keys Ibuki had tossed onto the table was mostly key chains. There was one shaped like a heart and another in the shape of the word *Ibiza*.

Judging from how deeply they were all asleep, Jackson guessed it must be later in the day than he'd thought. He looked at the clock and saw it was just before noon, then crept out of the hotel without waking anyone. On his bike ride home, he noticed the puma and kitsune embroidered on the sweats he was wearing.

Jackson dialed Ibuki. "Sorry! I took your pants," he said.

"Looks like it," Ibuki responded, laughing.

Jackson promised to return them when they met again next week. When he felt around in the pockets, he found a razor from the hotel. He laughed. *Even rich people do this kind of thing, I guess.*

THE NEXT FRIDAY, X, having searched through all their phone records again, reported that he'd still found nothing, as expected. No one pointed out that if there was nothing to discuss, he could have just messaged,

JACKSON ALONE

and instead they looked on cautiously as X seemed to let his guard down around them.

X did send, to Jackson alone, a single phone number. There were no numbers that they all shared, but that one, X explained, was in both his and Jerin's contacts. Jackson didn't recognize it but said he'd check it out.

They ordered pizza, and while Jerin went to pick it up, X moved his clothes to the safety of one of the nightstands, Jackson placed the razor that Ibuki had tried to take home next to the new one, and they each took turns in the shower. Between showers, they paced anxiously over the map of the world on the floor, the Ibiza key chain fell off the bed and onto India, and the room gradually grew messy. When Jerin returned with pizza, he felt sad, not because the room was in such a state of disarray but because the next morning it would all be gone.

After eating, they zoned out to the TV. Jackson wasn't really paying attention to what they were watching so much as staring at the backs of the other three men from the corner of one of the beds. They were all so at ease. Jackson wasn't especially eager to search for the criminal, either, but he sensed a vague danger in everyone beginning to lose their sense of purpose, like a faucet someone had forgotten to turn off.

"What is this 'We've switched places' crap?" X said, for a laugh, as he brought one of the remaining slices of pizza to his mouth. This Friday's TV movie was an anime, one where a high school boy and girl traded bodies.

"If you take away their hair and school uniforms, they've basically got the same face anyway," X said. "Do you guys like manga?"

Before X could turn to the others, Ibuki answered, "I hate it," which was enough to satisfy X, and he continued his tirade without waiting to hear from the other two.

"I hate it, too. It's like they draw a black line on a white piece of paper and say to themselves, *This is an outline of a person. This white part is skin. A human, just like us!* Anyone who genuinely buys that must have it so easy. Whenever I see that crap, really whenever it so much as comes into my line of sight, it makes me so unhappy. Don't they have more important things to do than draw their perfect pictures of food and sunsets? Everyone's going on about 'depressing anime' right now, but all anime and manga are depressing to me."

JACKSON ALONE

"Isn't that a little extreme?" Jerin said, letting out a gentle laugh through his nose. "Anime's not *that* racist. I've seen plenty of Black characters. And there's this thing called 'screentone,' where they can, like, use these little dots and, by adjusting the density, make tons of different skin shades, not just black and white." Jerin tried to sound casual in his counterargument, but he scrolled on his phone rapidly as he spoke, seemingly searching for something.

"Okay, so this screentone thing?" This time it was not X but Ibuki who cut off Jerin. "Why don't they use that on all the characters, then? They don't use it on the characters who're supposed to be Japanese. These bastards have transcended wanting to be white people. They wanna be white paper. And then they say *It's a global boom!* or *We won this prestigious European prize!* and get some trophy from a white dude and everyone celebrates. Who can stand that shit? I'm not even talking about the story or the politics. It's deeper than that. They're cheating on a fundamental level."

The words hit Jerin like bullets. Ibuki was no longer talking to Jerin, or about the show they were watching. He was on a tirade against anime and everything associated with it, and Jerin was merely caught in the cross fire. He had no way to respond.

Jerin thought about the manga he had saved on his phone. He had just landed a role in a play based on it. It was set in New York, and he was going to perform, in drag, double-cast alongside a female dancer, the part of a spy with a "dark complexion," who appears in a strip club at the beginning. Jerin wanted to brag, to tell them about how he was going to be onstage, but he figured they'd react about the same as if he were trying to lure them into a cult, so he gave up on the idea and shut off his phone screen.

But Jackson saw Jerin's screen from where he was sitting, and noticed that Jerin was antsy to say something. He also noticed that every time Ibuki spoke, the muscles on the back of his head tensed. Jackson didn't need to see Ibuki's face to know that he was fuming. It was strange for Ibuki to seize this opportunity to spit venom, his target changing rapidly, so rapidly that Jackson felt relieved to have X laughing it off next to him.

"I hate BL, too," Ibuki continued. "They're just stealing my viewers and don't do anything to support us. *This* is BL. The real deal."

"What does that mean?" Jerin said. "'Real deal'?"

JACKSON ALONE

"It means I'm actually living it. Not appropriating something for some porno make-believe."

Both on social media and in real life, Ibuki spoke on all topics with absolute confidence, but this exchange had turned into him trying to educate Jerin, and Jackson couldn't stand it. He couldn't shake the feeling that the weed cookies and the map game, their hotel-room meetings—that it was all some effort to groom them. And, that aside, why wasn't Ibuki helping more directly in their search for the culprit?

"Ibuki," Jerin said, "what does 'dark complexion' mean?"

Standing in the spotlight is a dancer of dark complexion, the script read.

Jerin showed him the line. He hadn't given up fully on talking about his play.

"It's a shit expression that intentionally lumps together Africans and Latinos and people who go to tanning salons."

That was it! Jackson yelled in response, "What if we *tra-ade pla-ces!*"

He'd done it on purpose, but still, Jackson's voice came out sounding so anime it embarrassed even him. After everyone boiled over with laughter, the room fell silent.

"I mean . . ."

"Should we try it?"

"It could be something."

After a moment, the commercials started and three shadows turned to Jackson, their ears and throats trembling. They made Jackson think of three Dobermans waiting for a command.

THOUGH THE FOUR had yet to identify the criminal, they'd concocted a plan for revenge and began practicing "trading places." First, Jackson would handle the checkout in Ibuki's place.

Before he left the room, Jackson made a final sweep to make sure no one had forgotten anything. He noticed that the new razor left out for them and the old razor Jackson had returned had both gone missing.

Checkout as Ibuki went so smoothly that next they got the staff to reissue the room key. Then came the taxi relay.

Jackson was first up. He hailed a cab, got in, and said to the driver, "Don't worry, I speak Japanese. Take the tunnel under the graveyard in front of the stadium and drop me off at Sendagaya Elementary."

JACKSON ALONE

Jackson got out, and immediately Jerin flagged down the same cab in front of the school.

"Don't worry," Jerin said to the driver, "I'm studying Japanese. Take the tunnel under the graveyard in front of the stadium to Yotsuya."

"I had another foreign customer just like you a second ago," the driver said, a bit unnerved, and when X got into the cab at the stadium and said, "Take the tunnel under the graveyard to Harajuku," the driver froze up. The second they made eye contact in the rearview mirror, he kicked X out of his cab.

Ibuki refused to be directly involved in the whole scheme, saying, "I've got a beard. And I'm so old I don't look like the rest of you," but he seemed happy to hear reports of their success.

These were harmless pranks meant to test the waters. But soon they moved to orchestrate revenge for Jerin.

Jerin had recently started dating a guy named Shun. Even outside the bedroom, Shun treated Jerin like his possession. When they ate out together, he'd make a point of commenting on Jerin's table manners. Loud enough that others could hear. When Jerin made even a small mistake speaking Japanese, Shun would poke fun at him as if those errors were not a matter of Jerin's Japanese proficiency but of his intelligence, and he'd correct Jerin in the sort of loud voice one would use talking to an old person. There was no way to get him to shut up. Jerin couldn't say anything to him, and Shun thought he was just doting on his boyfriend.

That night, Jerin and Shun had plans to meet up for a *yakiniku* dinner. Shun was pacing anxiously, in a two-meter radius, back and forth, in front of their meeting spot—irritated, because Jerin had not shown up yet and Shun was so used to calling the shots.

I'm close, Jerin texted. **Sorry, I took the wrong exit.**

He's not running late, Shun thought. He didn't even *try* to be on time.

From across the street, X could see Shun's paranoid delusions take hold of him. Then he felt Shun's eyes on him. X looked down at his phone and turned slowly in a circle to give Shun a full 360-degree view of his body. Once he confirmed that Shun was crossing the street toward him, he sat down on the guardrail. X listened as Shun's footsteps approached, then he felt a sharp slap against the phone in his hands. X loosened his grip and let the phone hit the ground.

JACKSON ALONE

"Can't you *read*?" Shun said coldly as X bent down to pick up the phone.

"Excuse me? What are you doing?" X asked the man ever so naturally. "Who are you?"

Upon hearing X's smooth Japanese pronunciation, Shun realized he'd made a huge mistake. But it was too late.

X grabbed Shun with all the righteous fury of someone who'd just had his phone slapped out of his hand. Shun lost his balance and began to fall, but X caught him by the necktie, shoved his foot into Shun's side, and stepped down with a force nearly capable of ripping an arm off his body. He pressed his foot down past the shirt, past the skin, through the subcutaneous fat, and straight through the ribs to his internal organs. X felt an unpleasant sensation, like he was crushing a long, narrow balloon beneath his foot. Passersby at first kept their distance to avoid getting involved, but once people started looking like they were searching for the right time to intervene, X put his whole weight onto Shun, stepped over him, and ran away. He took several odd turns, and when he stopped to check that he wasn't being followed, he felt the sweat flowing down his body begin to chill, and a smell wafted up from his armpits.

Jerin arrived soon after that and pretended he knew nothing. He apologized to Shun for being late, but Shun was no longer angry. He didn't say anything about having mistaken someone else for his lover, or, because of this error, having had his stomach smashed in.

"SO? WAS HE a changed man?"

"He was nicer than usual," Jerin said. "He didn't eat as much as usual. And when he came back from the bathroom, he massaged my shoulders."

On hearing that, the other three burst into a mix of cheerful cooing and disgusted laughter.

"That's actually kind of romantic."

"What's romantic about that?" X said. "I did all that so you could get your shoulders rubbed?"

"If he was the criminal, we could've gotten revenge."

"We could've."

"Maybe it's actually *more* logical for us to keep going for these little revenges instead of focusing on finding the one who did it," Jackson said, and everyone seemed

JACKSON ALONE

to agree. "But also," he continued, "we can't just go around hurting people. So we have to discuss whether each one's really necessary. Right?"

Jackson, who'd come up with the idea for this whole revenge plot, was the one to put a lid on it. But everyone nodded along seriously.

The conversation drifted to another topic, and eventually their attention turned to the hotel TV, on which an episode of *Lies and Pies* was playing. The four of them lay down using one another's bodies as pillows and watched.

"Wait. Don't they have to take a shot if they refuse to answer?" Jackson said, asking really the only thing he knew about the show.

"Oh, so about that rule. Someone who just kept answering 'No comment' had to be carried off in an ambulance, so they got rid of it. Now they just have the pie if you lose."

"They probably thought they were making it milder, but now it's just turned into a diss-off."

On this episode appeared the Black contestant who had recently said, "Most of the Black people in Harajuku are African. They're different from us Black Americans."

"This is gonna be your opponent, X?"

"Yeah. His name's Kiriyama Chris."

"Oooh. Now I'm excited."

THE NEXT MORNING when they left the hotel, they swapped outfits.

"There's a wallet in here. Should I take it out?" Jackson asked to no one in particular.

"Nah. If we switch all our wallets, it'll be even more confusing later on," Ibuki said.

"If I need anything, I'll pay with my phone anyway, and none of you know my PINs. It's fine. And I trust you," X added. Everyone expected him to be the most anal when it came to these sorts of things, so his answer put them at ease. If X said it was fine, it was fine.

Jerin put on Jackson's clothes and rode his bike home, too. He knew he could go fast if he pedaled harder, but he was apprehensive of the unfamiliar bike. After pedaling and then braking a few times, he ended up coasting most of the way home. He didn't feel at all like he'd truly become Jackson. He listened to the music he, as Jerin, had been listening to yesterday, and under his clothes, his sports bra was still squeezing his chest.

JACKSON ALONE

The possibility that they didn't naturally look alike but were *making* themselves look alike crossed X's mind on his own journey home. He was wearing Jerin's clothes, and while it wasn't his usual all-black look, X felt that the things he and Jerin looked for in clothing were actually pretty similar: Don't stand out too much but don't look too run-down. Wear something cool enough not to get condescended to but conservative enough not to get stopped by the police.

Ibuki wore X's clothes home. He stripped naked once he got back to his high-rise condo. X's underwear was a hand-me-down from Ibuki himself. Ibuki rarely gave his things away, but X was special. Once he'd started making his own money without relying on anyone else, Ibuki had found himself less able to sympathize with others. When he'd go out, he'd mentally block out anybody with lighter skin than his, as well as the men and women after the opposite sex, and when he did, the clubs in Roppongi were always empty. That was why, the night he'd met X, it had been so easy to find him.

Ibuki took an unused razor from the mountain of them in the bucket by his sink and slipped into the bathtub.

JOSE ANDO

He adjusted the angle of the circular mirror mounted by the tub, and for the first time in years brought a blade to his cheek. Under the sliding of the razor, his beard fell away just like a layer of grime and dissolved into the hot water. The bottom of the face that he'd grown so used to and had come to think of as true to him was pulled off like a mask, and a face just like Jackson's and the others' appeared.

Jackson didn't go straight home. He went to work and sent Jerin a photo. It was of their next target. Jerin carefully examined the photo as he lay in bed and streamed the seventh episode of one of his favorite anime. He'd first been drawn to this show—a cel animation created over twenty years ago—back when he was a child browsing the web for new anime to watch.

In each episode, the main character, i, is sent to a different country in a different time, where they must unravel the mysteries of a secret organization known as Σ. Every two episodes, the director changes so that the show constantly incorporates new styles and visuals from some of the most prominent creators in the animation and subculture worlds. i is not a human but a superdimensional intelligence made of liquid metal,

JACKSON ALONE

and their appearance changes in each episode. The only thing that remains constant is the female voice actor playing the role. Each time Jerin had arrived in a new country because of his father's job, the meaning and value of his face, too, would change—for Jerin, imagining himself as the reincarnation of i was his most intimate fantasy.

It was evening when Jerin awoke. As he watched the light drift around his hand, he saw that the mere outline he'd had last episode had been replaced with solid flesh and dark skin that clung to his nervous system. The world i was sent to this episode must have one more dimension than the previous ones, Jerin thought as he took notice of the two holes at the bottom of his nose. i discovered that that thing, which had just been a <-shaped line drawn on their face, was actually an organ meant for breathing in air.

Rumor had it that the actor who voiced i lived somewhere in Japan. Jerin had learned that she might occasionally shop at Lomero, so he'd decided to get a job there. When there were no customers and he had free time, he stared at the people passing by on the other side of the glass door and imagined the scene of her arrival. If she was still alive, she would be about the same age as his mother.

Oh, I've gotta go. Jerin ended his solo make-believe time and rushed off to Jackson's workplace.

He put an earphone in just one ear and played a song. *"I want to see myself the way you see me."* He modulated his throat to match the English lyrics. Out poured his voice, shaped by those modulations and filled with emotion. With a love song, he disarmed the tediousness of the wind and scenery passing him by as he pedaled.

Before falling asleep, he had checked the photo of the captain several times, and he spotted him among the other athletes immediately. He kept pace with about a block's distance between them and waited for the captain to break away from the others.

"You gotta go faster than you think you'll need to when you hit him. It'll actually be more dangerous if you don't. If you turn even a little, you've already lost. Go in like a punch. Hit him, then pull back. After you pull back, change directions." Following Jackson's advice, he rammed the captain from the side. Jerin was surprised by how little he felt the impact.

JACKSON ALONE

Ok, just finished, Jerin texted.

                                                You okay?

Yup

I don't think he saw my face either

                                                Awesome

You at work?

                          Yup. Gonna get a late lunch

Did anyone see you?

                                They will right now

After sending the last message, Jackson used the back of his hand to slowly topple his paper cup full of cocoa, sending it tumbling off the table. The brown liquid splashed across the floor. There were only a few people in the food court, and they were all either talking to one another or talking into their computers. But they reacted to the sound and recognized Jackson. Jackson showed no signs of guilt, chased away their gazes with his own glimmering eyes, and wiped Ibuki's sneakers with a paper napkin, cleaning off the small specks of cocoa splatter.

• • •

JOSE ANDO

JERIN WAITED FOR X in the grass behind the public toilet.

"X?"

"It's me."

"I couldn't tell who you were," Jerin said.

"It's about that time we disappear into the dark," X said with a laugh. The sun was low, but the sky was still blue, and their skin had developed a cold color as if that blue had begun seeping into it.

X put on Jackson's clothes, which Jerin had been wearing, then biked twenty minutes to a hotel much larger than Hotel Sagitari. He met Ibuki in the stall of a bathroom near the concierge desk. Ibuki raised his arms up like a child, and X pulled the turtleneck off him before taking off Jackson's T-shirt.

X adjusted his new clothing in front of the sink mirrors.

"It's not weird?"

"It looks good on you," Ibuki said. "Here, put this on, too." Ibuki unclasped the gold chain around his neck and put it on X.

"Check that out. Looking good."

"Wow, you're right," X said.

JACKSON ALONE

The lounge on the top floor was filled with fancily dressed people who applauded as the DJ and jazz band wrapped up their combined set. The beat from the house music alone continued as X took the stage. No one clapped for him.

"You're thinking I'm gonna sing, right?" he said. "I know, just look at me. But believe it or not, I can't hold a note to save my life!"

He spotted a few smiles in the audience but didn't hear a single laugh—they were all just smiling to be polite. No one was even looking at him.

"Japan is the country of *kotodama*, they say. The spirit of words. Recently I finally understood what that means. One day at the *konbini* I always go to there was this old man, he must've been in his sixties. Old enough that I think we can safely call him an old man. So he's working at the convenience store, and he's very, very kind to me, and extremely polite. When I hand over my money, he says, 'Thank you very much.' When he hands me the change, he says, 'Thank you very much.'

"It was only about three days after I first met this old man that I noticed something was up. That day, I hand him a curry plate and he says, 'Thank you very much.'

JOSE ANDO

He asks if I need a bag and I say no. 'Oh, is that so. Thank you very much. Shall I heat this up?' Yes, please. 'Thank you very much.' He puts the curry in the microwave. 'Thank you very much.'"

X turned to face the audience, his expression as blank as that of a Noh mask. He waited patiently for a handful of people in the mostly inattentive crowd to laugh. Once laughter began dribbling out of a few of them, then, finally, others began to pay attention.

"He zaps the bento in the microwave, and 'Thank you very much.' He takes down chopsticks from the rack, and 'Thank you very much.' He takes down an *oshibori*, and 'Thank you very much.' It was like he needed to say it every time he took a breath. I was starting to get creeped out."

The lounge bubbled with laughter.

"And then he handed me my change. 'Thank you very much.' I threw away the receipt. 'Thank you very much.' I thought to myself later that he must be going through a difficult time. Like, maybe this has something to do with some new self-actualization craze. If he's really bought into that kind of thing, you know, it's kind of sad.

JACKSON ALONE

"Have any of you ever worked at a convenience store? Probably not, I bet. That kind of work is for people like me, isn't it? It's really hard, you know. The pay sucks, you're always busy. It must've been hard on that old man, too. He must've been hoping for his life to take a turn for the better. When I asked him about it later, turned out he was the manager."

X gave the perfect subdued smile, and the crowd's laughter grew louder.

"Anyway, I just had one thing I wanted to say to all of you."

X faced the mic and stood up straight. *"Thank you very much,"* he said with a bow.

Ibuki laughed along with the crowd but felt it was so like X to chicken out and not roast himself a bit, too. To give himself something to do, he walked over to the buffet for a snack. He piled a plate with the leanest-looking cuts of meat and a piece of persimmon for dessert. When he returned to the table, a phone was vibrating. It wasn't his but X's, which he was holding on to. It was Jackson. After a moment of hesitation, Ibuki went to the elevator hall and answered the call.

"Sorry, X is onstage," he said. "Something wrong?"

"Nothing at all. It worked," Jackson said.

"That's great. So, what's up?"

"I found it. The number."

"The number?"

"You haven't heard from X?"

Jackson told Ibuki about the number X had asked him to investigate.

"No, I hadn't heard anything about that."

"I'd just looked through my personal phone," Jackson said, "but when I looked through the contacts on my work phone, which I never use, I found it."

"Really?"

"I really never use it, so I hadn't even thought about it."

"X never told me anything, so I don't know what to say. So, who was it?"

"I didn't save the number. I'm going to find out right now."

"But what are you going to say if they pick up?" Ibuki said.

"Something about my phone breaking? Whatever. I just need their name."

"That sounds like a plan. Be careful."

JACKSON ALONE

"Yup. Not sure how to be careful, but I'll try," Jackson said, laughing.

After hanging up, Jackson cleared his throat in the empty massage room. He coughed up some phlegm, then called the unknown number.

"Hello?" the voice on the other end said.

"Hello," Jackson said. "Sorry, my phone broke, so I'm trying to recover my contacts."

"The number you have dialed is the personal phone number of your boss, Eiji-san," Eiji said, playfully mimicking the voice of an automated recording. In the darkness of Jackson's mind, Eiji's face appeared as if illuminated by a spotlight.

"Don't you remember?" Eiji said. "That time I forgot my keys? I had you wait for me."

"Oh, that's right."

"That's why you have this number."

"Oh yeah."

"I don't think you'll need it, but maybe save it just in case."

"Will do."

"You've got a shift today?"

"That's right."

JOSE ANDO

The sound Eiji made in response reminded Jackson of a frog croaking beside a bog. It sounded like he was saying "Ahh," but with his mouth closed. Jackson had once heard that Eiji had studied abroad. Though Eiji had never said anything to suggest it, Jackson was convinced that sound must have been a habit from his time overseas.

Eiji's lips appeared in Jackson's mind. When pressed together, they stuck out and a crease formed behind them. He didn't like Eiji, but for some reason Jackson always remembered those lips.

4.

While Eiji wasn't Jackson's immediate superior, whenever Jackson saw him, he'd still bow his head and greet him with a smile. Eiji was fifteen years older than Jackson and always wore black leather sandals. He belonged to the department that oversaw all in-house operations at Athletius, and he was close with the managers of the gym and food court. Given that, all the staff who worked below the managers, like Jackson, clung to Eiji like his very existence linked them to the full-time Athletius employees.

Jackson had another connection to him. Eiji was the only one, out of ten interviewers, to have given Jackson's application a strong yes. Jackson had heard that directly from Eiji.

"I want to support the gays. I am one, too, after all," he said at lunch one day, surrounded by several other people. Eiji spoke plainly. He made no attempt to conceal what he was saying, and he wasn't making a show of it, either. He did seem a bit proud, though.

JOSE ANDO

Jackson didn't comment on the other reason Eiji had given for supporting him—that he was "rare." To Eiji, rarity was an important criterion with which to select people.

During the interview, Eiji immediately clocked Jackson as gay and set his sights on him. Approximately 10 percent of Japan's population identified as LGBTQ+; mixed-race people made up about 2 percent, and since Jackson was not half some-other-Asian or white, he must've been even rarer. He was young and inexperienced, but they were looking for cogs. Eiji thought that "good" and "bad" were more or less irrelevant categories when it came to cogs; the value of a cog came only from whether it fit perfectly into its groove. As Eiji grew older, this belief only intensified.

Eiji could've passed on his application, but at the end of the interview, Eiji decided to take a gamble. He asked Jackson a final question.

"By the way, Jackson," he said, "are you left- or right-handed?"

"Left."

He'd made up his mind. Eiji responded with that croak.

JACKSON ALONE

While Eiji could judge Jackson's work performance only based on what he heard from others, Jackson seemed to be doing relatively well.

But there came a time when Eiji's impression of Jackson began to change. It started with Jackson's first complaint.

> When I greeted ▇▇▇▇▇▇▇▇ in the morning, he told me 'Looking dark today, too' and laughed at me. This made me very uncomfortable. Will you please talk to him about his behavior?

Jackson didn't contact the gym manager or Eiji about this but emailed HR directly. Eiji heard about it later from the HR rep who'd received the complaint. By that time, the HR rep had already called Jackson and the other man in and had him apologize. As he reported this all to Eiji, the HR rep feigned distress but was excited like a rubbernecker watching an accident. Eiji could only imagine that what the other staff member had done was wrong, and replied, "Isn't Jackson in the right?" No other staff member was informed about that incident.

During his lunch break, Eiji went to mess around in

JOSE ANDO

the gym. He was concerned about how Jackson would be doing and was surprised to see just how cheerful he was. Jackson approached the other instructors, even the one who'd offended him, with smiles. Seeing that made Eiji even more anxious. Was he pretending there was no problem? Or had the apology been enough to reset their relationship in Jackson's mind?

Soon after, Jackson sent a few more emails to HR. Last week ▮▮▮▮▮▮▮ came for a massage appointment. He said to me, 'There are rumors that you're gay. Is it true?' This is a violation of my privacy, so I would like you to talk to him about his behavior.

▮▮▮▮▮▮▮, who came for an appointment on the same day, said, 'Black asses really are special,' and touched me inappropriately. I found this very uncomfortable and would like you to ban him from massage services.

These kinds of reports kept coming. Because the messages were incredibly blunt, it was impossible to parse what the atmosphere of the situation or what the intention on either side of the interactions was like.

[86]

JACKSON ALONE

The HR rep grew unsure about how seriously to take Jackson's emails. When he looked into the complaints, he found that they were all true, but the people being complained about had no ill intentions and were shocked to find that Jackson had ratted them out. As for Jackson, when HR listened to what he had to say, he didn't come off as especially angry but rather like he was calmly pointing out some sort of clerical error.

Jackson hadn't done anything wrong at all, but the HR rep seemed to be getting fed up with him. He started complaining to a few other people besides Eiji about this, describing the whole thing with a mix of confusion and amusement.

At first Eiji regarded those who were made to apologize to Jackson with genuine disdain and felt no pity for them, but their numbers continued to increase, and one day he felt his perspective shift as though he'd been struck by a sudden bout of vertigo. There goes Jackson, he thought. Filing yet another complaint.

Eventually, in the office smoking room, Eiji put into words what the HR rep and those who'd been complained about were probably thinking but couldn't say themselves. He'd meant it as mere lip service to his

JOSE ANDO

neutrality, but as the words left him, he felt a weight lift off his chest. "Why doesn't he just *talk* to them?"

When he checked in on Jackson, he was always smiling, never showing any signs of distress. One time, he was hiding behind the counter, blowing up balloons for a surprise party for one of the staff members from his training group. Another time an employee who came for a massage asked to add him on LINE and he did so enthusiastically. He always looked so defenseless and friendly that it was like he was setting a trap.

Eiji's image of Jackson as a person began to split. The Jackson he witnessed himself was charming, but the Jackson whose name he heard in rumors made him imagine a pitch-black bug. A single vermin, spotted all throughout the company, that could flit about as if by magic. Eiji wasn't sure what he'd do if he ever encountered that insect.

One day, he decided to talk to Jackson about it. That night after most of the employees had gone home and Jackson was alone cleaning the gym, Eiji called him over and took him for coffee. Eiji talked about his own experiences first, about how when he'd first joined the company, he couldn't come out; about studying abroad; about finally getting results here and having

JACKSON ALONE

his accomplishments recognized. He sprinkled in some laughs but bared it all for Jackson as he told his story.

Jackson had heard Eiji's story before, when they'd gone out drinking together, but he listened and reacted as though he were hearing it for the first time.

"I'm sure it wasn't easy for you when you were a kid, either," Eiji said. "I'm sure you faced adversity."

"Yeah, I guess so."

"And so I wondered what was going on."

"Hmm?"

"The HR complaints. Do you ever tell them what you're thinking or feeling when you're actually in one of those situations?"

"Depends, I guess. Depends on the situation."

"But you want to tell HR about it?"

"You know, it just never ends," Jackson said.

"It's not just about how you feel in the moment?"

"What?"

"Whether to tell HR, for example. Whether you'll let this person get away with making some comment, but you don't want this other person to say the same thing."

"Am I not allowed to have feelings?"

"No, that's not what I'm saying. It's just that the company can't make guidelines that way. You don't want everyone to treat you like a problem, do you?"

"I guess not."

"Can you tell me how you felt when someone said something rude to you?"

"Hmm."

"All you say is 'Hmm.' Put it into words," Eiji said, laughing.

"Well, I don't think my feelings have anything to do with it." As he said this, Jackson sounded as though he were reading from a script.

There it is, Eiji thought. That attitude, it's not fair. It all made sense to Eiji now. If Jackson's feelings were actually irrelevant, if Jackson had just approached everyone in this robotic, unfeeling way, that would've prevented all this "harm." So, then, why was he always acting in this half-assed friendly way? Most of the people who said inappropriate things did so only because they wanted to befriend Jackson, and if they misread their closeness, it was the least Jackson could do, would just be the polite thing to do, really, to tell them a little about how he felt. To say that he was embarrassed, or

JACKSON ALONE

bothered, or upset. Just one word. He wanted to get just *one* word about how Jackson hurt.

The growing distance Eiji felt between himself and Jackson had nothing to do with Eiji's own history. Long before that trivial division had formed between them, Eiji had been buying men, using them in the most shocking ways, and filming it. To Eiji, that was neither an uncommon desire nor one with its lack of sympathizers. He'd created a social media account under the username Groundwater and now followed close to a thousand men and had almost four thousand followers. His feed was inundated with men having sex. What those users had done to other men, what had been done to them, they reported it all ravenously with videos and photographs. That Eiji was married, that what he did was borderline criminal—none of this was uncommon. This was a world in which, rather than the beauty of appearances or the correctness of claims, the unspeakable had value. So when Eiji saw a post saying **fucked a college jock till his bussy broke**, Eiji also wanted to fuck "a college jock till his bussy broke." No matter how extreme the kink was, he felt this need to mimic what he saw on his feed. When he found out about man-howling, when he saw that the act had amassed over 120,000 likes, Eiji lusted after this new violence.

If he ever got threatened by one of the men he'd preyed upon, he told himself he'd be fine deleting his entire account. This was all just for fun and he could do it all over again, as many times as he wanted.

Back when he was having trouble with Jackson, he'd just so happened to hire a boy named Adam who looked uncannily like him. He thought to himself, I finally have something on Jackson. Eiji found that the pursuit of his escapist fantasies had actually brought him slamming back into reality, and that discovery affirmed him in his course of action.

When Eiji finally met Adam in person, Adam appeared, at first, to both recognize Eiji's face and not know it at all, but gradually it became clear to Eiji that Adam didn't know him. This disappointed Eiji. Then it excited him. It meant he could do whatever he wanted. Eiji said he'd pay double if Adam agreed to meet in secret without going through the agency.

Unlike many other kinds of sex play, man-howling was surprisingly easy to set up. Other boys had agreed to Eiji's double-pay offer, so he summoned them to a

JACKSON ALONE

soundproof rental playroom. For some reason, though, Adam kept turning down his private invitations, so Eiji contacted the agency and reserved him and carried the mic and rented speaker and his own bondage belts to a corner room in Hotel Sagitari, where he then invited Adam.

"What did it feel like?" Eiji asked Adam after untying him.

But Adam hardly said anything about the pain. That inability to put things into words also reminded Eiji of Jackson. Though they were different people, the way they followed the same patterns of behavior invited the assumption that their likeness stemmed from something in their shared background.

They had other things in common as well. When asked for something, their faces both froze into an unhappy look for a moment. But once you made the slightest effort to win them over, they caved so easily. When he talked to Jackson while he was cleaning, when he got Adam to take the drugs—both times, it was like that. However many times they experience the same pain, they resist in the same way, Eiji once thought to himself, yet, ultimately, they demonstrate the same obedience.

Have these people, by their very nature, been robbed of their capacity to problem solve? Or, Eiji imagined, maybe they have an incredibly strong predisposition to subservience. His hypothesis quickly transformed into conviction: He knew that must be the truth.

Eiji, as Groundwater, released the video on his private account. He immediately received a few messages and sold the unedited and uncut version to several people. Maybe he'd sell more, or maybe it would start circulating beyond his control before then. It didn't matter either way.

He dreamed of countless Jacksons multiplying in number and fell into a deep sleep.

*

ON SATURDAY MORNING, Eiji went through his normal routine with his partner, Ken. Ken lied, saying he had four appointments in a row that morning at his part-time job as a gym instructor, but then headed to the home of a man he'd met on an app. Eiji lied, too, saying he'd be home, but then went for a massage. In the afternoon, Ken actually went to his job, and Eiji was actually at home browsing Instagram on the account he kept under his real name.

JACKSON ALONE

Eiji's feed was filled with gay parents. He knew there had always been same-sex couples raising kids, like them, but ever since a certain nonfiction web manga had gone viral, he'd started to see so many of them that he had to wonder where the hell they'd all been hiding. Among all the posts, he spotted a couple he'd seen long before. It was seeing their posts that had first made him think he could raise a child, too. And then, ten years ago, they'd decided to adopt Yuni.

As for Ken, his Saturday noon classes were always full. He apologized to those who couldn't get in, then closed the glass door behind him. There were the students, waiting with their yoga mats spread out on the floor. Students who, an hour later, flowed out of that room after it had transformed into a sauna. Then the sound of iron clanging against iron. A man making a complaint to the staff in the changing room. Footsteps. A man talking into his AirPods while lathering his body with lotion.

"That was the first time anyone did that to me. It was like an alien parasite was growing in my stomach," the man said. "Yeah, but I've never heard anyone say anything about hearing a voice from inside your own body when you're giving birth. It really was abnormal.

So mechanical. That's why I said no, but I was drugged. Yeah, he's a freak. Yeah, yeah, I'm fine. I plan to make him apologize. I'll tell his partner. If it comes to it, I'll tell that adopted kid of his. I've decided I'll ruin his life if I have to. I can't let someone like that be a dad."

Ken stole a glance at the man. Skin he associated with violent crime, beautifully shaped eyes (the one thing that, Ken had to admit, he was a little jealous of), arms and legs thinner than Ken's own Asian ones. Ken identified several things about the man that confirmed he was inferior, and once reassured, Ken shut up his thoughts on the topic.

People avoided walking near that man, so a space formed around him. Of course there was a space. He was a dangerous man talking about dangerous things. What is he talking about? Ken wondered. But if he looked at him, they'd almost certainly make eye contact, so Ken rushed out of the changing room.

In the afternoon, Yuni would come home from her club activities and she and Ken would play video games together. He'd wake her up just as she started nodding off. This was how their weekends always went.

Ken went to get the train. On the opposite platform

sat a man whose beauty he began to envy. Then he realized he was probably the same race as the man at the gym; he reminded himself the man was inferior, and calmed down.

Actually, though, *is* that the same guy from before? But I left the gym before him, and when I got to the station, he was already sitting there, Ken thought. And on top of that, this man had a different vibe. He had sunglasses on, and his skin shone as though varnished. From the movement of his lips, Ken imagined he was speaking a foreign language.

After the express train passed and the platform quieted down, Ken's gaze shifted again to the man, and to the odd movements he was making. He mimed gripping something in front of his stomach, then his hands moved up to his head as though he were trying to show that something was wailing inside of it. Where the eyes behind the translucent black of his sunglasses were looking, Ken couldn't tell. Which meant that there was a possibility he was looking straight at Ken. Upon realizing this, Ken turned away. The word *alien* came to him clearly, and the rest of what the man said dissolved into the air, leaving Ken unable to make it out.

JOSE ANDO

In the evening, he took Yuni to *juku*. After dropping her off, he gave the car to Eiji, who said he wanted to go for a drive. Near the station was a large shopping center and an amusement park. Ken took his dress shoes to get resoled, then headed for the sandwich shop Buns with Best Cheese. He passed through a scene from the near future and then crossed a bridge that led to a worn-down shopping district before arriving at the quiet shop. The tables and counters were all blackened with decades of use, and though it was a Saturday evening, the shop was empty. Ken could see an unenthusiastic-looking waiter and, on the other side of the counter, the top few centimeters of a man's head. He took a seat in a four-seater booth and ordered his favorite, the chicken burger.

"That was the first time anyone did that to me," a voice said. "It was like an alien parasite was growing in my stomach."

Ken froze as though caught in sleep paralysis. He didn't need to look to know it was the same man as before. He shoved the chicken burger down his throat to try and get out of there as fast as he could.

"He's already here."

They were talking about him. Ken's heart froze, and

JACKSON ALONE

though he tried to run from the shop, before he could get up, a man slid into the bench across from him and sat down. The unfriendly waiter seemed to have gone to check something in the back of the shop. Ken called out for help, but X began speaking, warmly, to shut him up.

"You're Eiji's partner, right?" he said.

"Who are you?"

"I'm Adam," X said.

"And? Who *are* you?"

"Eiji's victim."

"What do you mean 'victim'? You're just someone he had some fling with or something."

X extended his phone to Ken.

It started with a scream. In the video, Adam was tied up. Ken had seen each of the tools being used and sensed immediately that the things Eiji had done to him long ago, half in jest, were all practice for this.

Ken leaned back in his seat, impudent. The cushion made a weak noise as it gave under his weight. "Okay. And?" he said.

"Well, I'd hoped you'd be a little more shocked," X said, laughing. "This is your child's father!"

JOSE ANDO

"I'm so over this whole morality-police thing."

"What do you mean?"

"Adam, do you think any of the gays in the generations before us were actually fit to be parents?" Ken laughed, but it sounded like he was crying.

"'The gays' is too broad. I can't answer that."

"You can, though. No. The answer is no. Come on. Not a single one of them ever thought about living this kind of life. If you dig into anyone's past, you're bound to find something. Hiding whatever it is you find, that's actually the right thing to do."

"Please save the apologia for when Yuni gets here."

"What?"

"What time does *juku* finish again? Six?"

"If you so much as lay a finger on her, I will kill you," Ken said.

"I'm here, so I can't lay a finger on her. Not unless I learn how to astral project."

"What do you want from me?"

From the dusty tortoiseshell pen stand next to the window, X took a ballpoint pen made to look like a pencil and dashed off the number 110 on a paper napkin.

JACKSON ALONE

"Call. Help us provide evidence."

Ken was silent for a moment, then picked up his phone like he was trying to get something irritating over with as quickly as possible, and called. He glared silently at X for a moment and, though on the verge of tears, let out a frantic burst of words.

"Eiji, go get Yuni. Now," Ken said.

"Negotiation's over, then," said X.

"Ken?" Eiji said. "Is someone with you?"

"Adam."

Upon hearing that name, Eiji understood.

"Ken, calm down," he said. "Take a deep breath."

"Don't talk to me like that. Just go get Yuni now."

The call ended with the sound of something being severed with tremendous force. Eiji rushed to the *juku*, but Yuni was already gone. He ran to the park. He saw the fence, and in the middle of the futsal court illuminated by blinding lights, dressed in their fancy colors, flailing violently, their young voices blurring together, were the children dancing for a camera. He found Yuni among them and yelled, "Yuni!"

"Let me do one more take," Yuni said.

"We have to hurry home today. Let's go."

JOSE ANDO

Yuni came running. Seeing those graceful movements impossible for an adult to recreate, Eiji thought Yuni just might have been faster than him. Yuni never complained, just drifted along easily. Eiji took a deep breath and ducked under the green net.

"Ei-kun, why are you so on edge?" Yuni asked.

Their surroundings looked peaceful, and there was no sign of Adam, no trace of Jackson. Yuni ran ahead of Eiji and, stepping into the road, pointed left and then right.

"Which parking lot?"

"To the right. Don't run."

Before Yuni could escape, Eiji grabbed on to her hood, then pretended to dust it off.

THE EXCITED CLAMOR from just a moment ago had died down. Though anxious, Jackson kept his feet completely still as a police officer crouched next to him, shining a light on his bike.

He'd been biking around the area, ready in case X contacted him, until a minute ago, when he was stopped by the police.

"Please turn on your light."

JACKSON ALONE

"Of course."

He turned on the bicycle light and bowed slightly as he readied his feet on the pedals, but the officer waved his hands in front of him to stop him from moving.

"Actually, excuse me. Stop, please."

The officer guided Jackson closer to him with gestures even more exaggerated than his words, as though he were handling a child.

"How sad," said some middle-aged man who was watching everything from the sidelines. "Getting stopped just for not being Japanese."

"That has nothing to do with it. What are you suggesting?" the officer said, his voice taking on a performatively defensive tone, the syllables dragging out oddly.

"Standard procedure for the Japanese police," Jackson whispered to the man. It was just a quick comment, so Jackson wasn't sure how much the man actually heard, but a look of relief spread over his face and he crossed the street.

As the man left, the officer barked after him: "Should I stop you instead?"

"That's not right, is it?" Jackson said, making his eyes look as childishly innocent as possible. "That's basically

JOSE ANDO

acknowledging that you stop and search people just 'cause you feel like it, right? And saying that you can use that authority as a kind of punishment? That would mean that what that guy just said was the truth."

The officer's face clouded over. He tried to say something, but before he could, Jackson gave him his last name, got off the bike, and, pointing to the bicycle registration sticker, said, "Here."

The officer crouched down. Only then did Jackson remember that he was dressed as Jerin. He felt a nervous sweat coming on.

"Confirmed."

"All right." If Jackson tried to rush off, the officer would just grow more suspicious of him, so Jackson looked him in the eye and bowed.

"It gets dark at night. There's a chance you'll cause an accident or get into one. Please don't forget to turn on your light."

Instead of protesting, instead of telling the officer he didn't need the lights on because it was still light out, that he didn't forget but just didn't need them, Jackson repeated, "All right."

"Do you really understand?"

JACKSON ALONE

"What?"

"I know you're in a hurry, but what you were doing was actually very dangerous," the officer said. "Can you please pay attention to what I'm saying?"

"I'm sorry."

"All right. Can I please see your ID?"

Jackson stuck his hand in his pocket. He immediately felt Jerin's wallet. Should he say he'd forgotten his wallet entirely, or should he lie and say he had the wallet but no ID? He risked it and pulled it out.

"And your zairyu card?"

Jackson checked the contents of Jerin's wallet. He couldn't find anything that looked like a foreign residence card.

"I don't have it with me," Jackson said.

"Okay. Your passport, then."

"I'm not planning on going overseas."

"What?" The officer was now audibly irritated.

"I was just out for a ride, so I don't have it."

"If you don't have any ID, then I have to arrest you. If you don't want that, you need to cooperate."

"Cooperate? I said I don't have anything on me."

"Is that your wallet?"

The officer pointed at the wallet, so Jackson shut up and handed it to him.

"The name on your bank card doesn't match the name you gave for the bike."

"The bike is my friend's."

"You didn't mention that before."

"You didn't ask. If I had tried to explain, you would've just reacted the same way you are now. Isn't it all the same in the end?"

"Can you contact the owner of that bike right now?" the officer said.

"If he doesn't pick up, then what happens?"

"That's up to me," said the officer, who seemed to be speaking not so much to Jackson but to all the passersby.

Jackson called Jerin, but he didn't pick up.

"He won't answer."

"All right. Then leave the bike here and get in my car. We'll go to your home and I'll have you show me your zairyu card. This is your last chance."

When Jackson checked his phone in the car, he saw messages from Jerin.

Sorry, I was asleep

Are you okay?

JACKSON ALONE

Come on, get it together, Jackson thought, angry for a moment.

Just tell me your address

Jackson's message was blunter than usual.

The car was at a large intersection. If it turned right, it would head in the direction of Jackson's actual home, but it continued straight, and Jackson began to see more and more unfamiliar buildings. A sense of hopelessness overtook him as he realized he'd have no way of knowing if the cop was tricking him and taking him to a totally different address.

They arrived at the door of Jerin's apartment, which Jerin had promised to leave unlocked. When Jackson turned the knob nervously, the door opened, and his chest tightened for a split second. Jerin was standing there in the darkness, hiding in the corner of his entryway, his face so serious. When Jackson saw him, he grew even angrier. He turned his eyes away from Jerin's face and took the zairyu card.

Satisfied, the officer headed back to his patrol car. Jackson wanted to shout *What about the bike?*

"Are you okay?" Jerin asked.

"What?"

JOSE ANDO

"I just . . ."

"I already explained it to you. About the ID."

"Look. You didn't have my zairyu card, so that cop was mean to you. I'm sorry. You're mad at me, not your unluckiness?" Jerin said. "That could've happened to me, too. I could've needed help. But here I was, asleep, like it has nothing to do with me."

Those were the very words making their way up Jackson's throat, which he'd been ready to fling at Jerin. *What if it had been you?* But, somehow, hearing them from the mouth of the man himself, Jackson felt an inexplicable shock. Jackson hugged Jerin.

Jackson felt he had to say something to Jerin, to mend something he had broken. But Jerin started to speak first. "I didn't forget to give you the card. I just can't lend it to anyone, so I held on to it."

"Jerin, you're the most put together of us."

"Yeah, and now I guess I'm finally on the same level as the three of you."

"So now what?"

"I'm ready to just go back to having normal fun."

Jerin's voice remained soft. Normal fun. Come to think of it, Jackson had never had normal fun. Just

JACKSON ALONE

abnormal fun. That meant that to Jerin this whole mission, all of this, was just for fun. To Jerin, who didn't have citizenship in this country, this was all just some extravagant game. Jackson had no choice but to accept that. He couldn't say anything else about it. Finally, Jackson kissed him. Jerin's lips pushed back. Jackson tried to grab on to Jerin's hands, but they remained loosely clenched and did not squeeze back. This time it truly felt like Jackson was touching his own anesthetized hands.

They said they'd be in touch, and Jackson left the apartment.

5.

The Monday after their failed revenge plot, Eiji showed up at the Athletius gym as usual. Just as he'd done every Monday before, he visited after lunch and made his rounds, checking in with all the staff. He stopped to talk with several people chatting at the reception desk, then, on his way back to his office, his gaze turned to Jackson's massage room.

Jackson pretended to focus on the massage he was giving while he prayed for Eiji to vanish. But Eiji remained facing him, and several other sets of eyes in the vicinity were turned toward Jackson as well, awaiting his reaction.

Jackson screwed up the courage to turn his attention to the reception desk, as though he'd just noticed Eiji's presence. Just as their eyes fully met, Eiji waved to him and left the gym.

Eiji had forced Jackson into an armistice. Given his crimes, Eiji couldn't confront Jackson publicly; Eiji also knew Jackson was in the same position. They'd keep up pleasantries despite their mutual distrust, and they'd maintain their distance so as not to encroach on the other's territory. This had now been stipulated by Eiji. It was all decided almost too smoothly.

Jackson tried to squeeze some anger out of his body, but the truth was there might never have been any to begin with. It felt as though the blood he was certain had been pumping through his body until at least that night had been replaced with air. Jackson's body simply floated through the usual brightness and sleepiness of the afternoon like a swollen balloon. His fingers felt fuzzy. He squeezed them and worked the blood flow, as though trying to wake something up.

Jackson kept this a secret from the other three, but he was actually relieved he'd been stopped that night. If he'd gotten the go-ahead from X after that, Jackson wasn't sure he'd have been able to confront Eiji head-on, pretend to be Adam and question him, or even worse, come at him from behind and harm him before he was recognized. He might've just run away.

When he thought about why he couldn't direct his hatred at Eiji, he remembered Eiji's lips the first time they'd met.

JACKSON ALONE

Eiji had complimented him during his interview. The following week, an email arrived saying that he'd been hired. That was all. That was their entire relationship, so why had he been robbed of his power to be angry? Eiji's lips the first time Jackson saw him. Eiji, who didn't say anything until the very, very end of the interview, had kept his lips pressed together tight the whole time Jackson was answering questions. There was a crease behind Eiji's lips. In his mind, Jackson talked shit: What's with this guy's mouth? He's so full of it. He was sure Eiji was bored, but then suddenly at the end, he complimented Jackson, said he wasn't like anybody else, and Jackson wasn't sure how to respond. He wanted to know when Eiji had started to like him. No matter how many times he replayed the interview over in his head, he was never sure. He was never sure when his power had been taken away.

If Eiji hadn't been someone who once so unhesitatingly recognized Jackson despite him having nothing to show, Jackson could've killed Eiji, could've confronted him to his face, maybe. Maybe he would've immediately reported him to HR, like he did with the other staff, and maintained the distance between them. But it was too late for that. Jackson didn't have the courage to see as an enemy someone who'd once shown him kindness.

"Jackson, do you get along with Eiji?"

Zen was lying face down on the massage table. He'd been talking about something this whole time, and while Jackson was sure he'd been responding, he was only now actually conscious of Zen's presence. Surely, on some level, he'd buried his sympathy for Zen just as he had for the other staff members. When he thought about it, this was the first time Zen had come to visit him since that day.

"What's the deal with you two?" Zen asked.

"No, we're not friends."

"I thought so. I could see it just now."

"Actually, I just recently realized I don't really like him."

"'Cause when someone likes you," Zen said, "you lose your ability to tell what you really think about them."

"Exactly what I was thinking."

"Who do you get along with here?" Zen asked.

"Who knows."

"Even I must be pretty high up there, just talking to you like this."

"I dunno."

JACKSON ALONE

"Or maybe you actually hate my guts."

"Well, it seems like you like me, so, you know . . ." Jackson laughed.

"Your judgment is failing."

"Yup."

"Uh-oh."

The pair's laughter was as flat as old soda. Before the remaining agreeableness faded, Jackson slapped Zen on the lower back to signal that the massage was over. He could tell that Zen wanted something more from him, but there was nothing else Jackson could open up to him about. The rest of the story was not Jackson's alone to tell.

YET ANOTHER FRIDAY came. Jackson had the day off. He checked the Hotel Sagitari app for open rooms and debated whether he should invite the others. He wound up looking at a totally different thing and fell asleep. When he woke up, it was already evening, and Jackson remembered that the newest episode of *Lies and Pies* was out.

Jackson and the other three all watched "Kiriyama

JOSE ANDO

Chris Questions Adam" in different locations at different times.

JERIN LISTENED ON his AirPods as he cooked. His boyfriend would be coming back from an overseas business trip soon. He'd told Jerin that he wanted to play house, so Jerin had searched Airbnb for a place with a fancy kitchen and booked it on his boyfriend's card.

Jerin glanced at his phone screen. A drone-mounted camera flew silently over the backs of the audience's heads, then over a pool, before showing the stage where Adam and Kiriyama Chris sat facing each other. It looked like the poolside of some hotel.

X had introduced himself as Adam in his first episode, "Adam Questions Lala." These few weeks after their plan had failed, no one had been in contact. So seeing the name Adam again for the first time in a hot second made Jerin think back to all that had happened.

Don't forget the salt, Jerin reminded himself. He'd been looking for the salt for a while now. He dug through the cabinet.

• • •

JACKSON ALONE

UNLIKE THE AMERICAN version, *Lies and Pies Japan* wasn't filmed in a studio but by a hotel pool. Adam and Chris sat facing each other, bathed in the light from a pool so blue it looked like the color had been painted on. Behind them was a glass-walled kitchen, inside of which several chefs darted about, paying no mind to the filming, skewers of churrasco on their grills.

Chris began the conversation. "It seems like a very important topic that a certain video of you has made the rounds."

"Sort of a forced way to put it."

"That video is connected to the clothes you wore in your behind-the-scenes audition video, right?"

"That's right. And? What's your question?"

"I'm not going to ask about the video."

"Am I supposed to thank you for that?"

"Why the combativeness?"

"I mean, this is a competition."

"Adam," Chris said. "I talked to your father."

"My father?"

"Yeah."

The camera closed in on Adam's smile frozen stiff like a mask. Groans traveled through the crowd. The audience's voices were apparently added in post, and it sounded as though they cycled through only a handful of options: laughter, either a roar or a hushed ripple; shouts; and groans. The intentionally cheap direction made the contestants seem like toys.

"Hey, Chris-san," Adam said. "I'm already twenty-one."

"What does that have to do with anything?"

"I mean, holding a full-grown adult's parent hostage? How dirty a move is that?"

Laughter erupted from the audience.

"I thought your dad might've had something to do with your over-defensiveness."

"Over-defensiveness?"

"You're always so hostile."

"Can you give me an example?"

"Your last episode," Chris said.

"Which part?"

"I don't want to repeat what you said. They've got the clip ready, so look at that screen over there."

JERIN, WHO WAS still at work in the kitchen and hadn't been listening closely, looked at his phone as if

JACKSON ALONE

directed by Chris's words. When the screen by the poolside lit up, X's thick and breathy voice rang pleasantly in Jerin's ears.

Several of X's lines from "Adam Questions Lala" had been cut up and rearranged, and were played back rapid-fire:

"I'm sorry to hear about your child, Lala . . . But, and I'm sorry to say this, I can't tell your kid apart from any other random kid running around on the street . . . Whether it's your kid with your partner, whoever they are . . . The kid you had with your sidepiece, the kid you and your partner borrowed someone's uterus to have, whatever, they're all basically just . . . They're the same, right? . . . Yeah, I'm sorry, but there's nothing special about that . . . Everyone loves news about a dead child . . . It *is* gross . . . You realize you only feel pity for your own kind, right?"

When the replay suddenly cut off, the crowd went wild.

"It's hard to even listen to," Chris said.

"You're the one who played it."

"I'll get to my main point soon, but you come off as so pitiful. I'm also part Black, so I understand; it feels hopeless. But you're just too . . ."

JOSE ANDO

"I don't want to hear any of this 'my brother' BS from someone who said that the Black people in Harajuku who try and make you buy clothes are mostly Africans, not Americans."

The audience laughed.

THERE WERE GRILL marks on the whitefish, so Jerin added white wine and let it simmer. He took a deep breath to calm the racing in his chest. From those few days of playing Adam, Jerin still carried with him an anxiety that any criticism of Adam was also criticism of him.

"SINCE YOU'RE JUST gonna keep hiding in your shell," Chris continued, "I'll play another video."

On the screen appeared a middle-aged Japanese man.

"Are you X's father?"

"Yes," the man said.

"Who is X?"

"That's his real name. It's a much better name than Adam, right?"

"Where did that name come from?"

JACKSON ALONE

"A famous Black American hero."

A peal of laughter from the crowd.

"Why did you decide to write X's name as 十字, with the kanji for *cross*?"

"I wanted to put some Japanese soul into it."

The audience had stopped laughing at X's father's obviously sincere answers and slipped, for a moment, into a mortified silence.

As X stared at his father on the screen, a fire burned in his belly. His father continued to answer interview questions: "My son's mother was irresponsible. She gave up on raising him and returned to her home country. I raised him in her place. Bringing him up, I made sure to respect his individuality. A *randoseru* didn't suit him, so I sent him to school with a normal backpack . . ." X's father seemed proud, but each time he spoke, the beads of sweat coating X's forehead grew thicker. He closed his eyes in an attempt to forget his entire existence. He focused on the pulsing color of the blood behind his eyelids and waited for the interview to end. Each time he clenched his jaw, there was a rumbling sound in his ear.

• • •

JOSE ANDO

"IT SEEMS LIKE there's a problem with your relationship with your father," Chris said.

"If you project an average, grubby, middle-aged man on a giant screen, that's gonna look pretty pitiful, and if my dad looks pitiful, then it's gonna look like we have issues. That's all."

"Let's watch the rest."

X'S FATHER JUST kept talking, even without getting asked any questions.

"I always vaguely knew that he was gay," he said. "I would be so happy if he brought home a boyfriend one day. I would celebrate that. And I can promise that proudly, with my head held high. I mean, I was ready to protect him from any discrimination whatsoever when I was raising him. But my son cares too much what other people think, that's just his personality, so he must've been embarrassed. And I am what I am, an imperfect parent."

No, you're wrong, X screamed inside. I just hate the way you try to make everything into a beautiful little story.

• • •

JACKSON ALONE

JERIN WAITED FOR the grape tomatoes to cook through. It was hard to understand all the talk about X's dad, so he didn't pay much attention, but the fact that he probably didn't get along well with X came through clearly. Jerin was drawn back to the show by Adam's voice saying, "Fine, I'll tell you about it."

"WE DON'T HAVE to watch till the end?" said Chris.
"We certainly don't."
"Well, then, let me ask a question about this."
"You want to know how my family complex led to my combativeness?"
"So you admit it?"
"Sure, I admit it. But that's all pretty normal. There's actually a much more important tipping point."
"The root of your over-defensiveness?"
"Yes. There's something else I'm far more scared of. Something worse than other people's opinions."
"What is it?"
"Blades."
"Is that why you've been holding on to something this whole time?"

JOSE ANDO

"That's right."

"Ha ha. Don't stab me, okay?"

"Ha ha ha. Don't worry. I'm just scared to have someone take it away from me, that's why I'm holding it. I guess this is a churrasco knife?"

"Sounds right."

"It's serrated."

"Keep talking."

"This story starts about two years ago. I'll give the rough summary. There are shady places out there for gay men to fuck."

The crowd laughed.

"This is no laughing matter."

Silence.

"Anyway, a famous Black mixed kid got beaten up in one of those shady places. In a private room. The man he was with just laid into him, and he carved something into his skin with a knife. And then someone else found him there unconscious, and everyone fled the scene. To be expected. Pretty much no one wants to be found going to that kinda place. The assailant slipped into the crowd and escaped. That spot is still there. They opened back up right away. You see it in the movies all the time, right? The scene where there's a gunshot and all the birds fly away. The men ran away like that, and, after a little while, they settled right back on the same tree. I mean, it's not like I don't get it."

"This is a real absorbing story. Assuming it's real."

"It's real."

"Okay? Say it is. I don't get how any of this is related."

"It's all about the word that was carved into him."

A muffled scream rose from the audience.

JERIN BROUGHT HIS face up close to the phone as Adam lifted his shirt. The bare chest that Adam was exposing to the cameras belonged to Ibuki, not to X. He pointed to a spot where his tattoos came together. The camera zoomed in. It was blurred out for the broadcast.

"CHRIS, CAN YOU read what this says?"

"You're too far away," Chris said. "I can't make it out."

"Here, I'll come closer. Give me your pointer finger. I'll move your hand. Follow the swollen part, the part that feels like a welt."

"I can't say this out loud."

The audience's silence continued.

"This . . . this is terrible," Chris said.

"I know, right?"

"I'm sorry. I'm gonna forget we're on this show for a second and say this. This, this is a good reason."

"For what?"

"For the extreme comments you made."

"But who is 'you'?"

The crowd stirred, and the applause built slowly.

"Chris, you still haven't noticed? Really look at my body. Now try to remember the guy in the video."

Ibuki, playing Adam, said this slowly, as though he were instructing him in pronunciation. Laughter spread through the audience as they began to realize the trick, and finally Chris raised his hands to the back of his head. A man wearing a hat came down from the audience and approached the stage. Engulfed in cheers of surprise, X removed his hat and quickly fixed his hair with his fingers. The audience went wild.

"Basically, the man in the video could've been someone else, as could that man playing my father. We can't know everything. The only thing we know is that there's a dad out there with no concern for his son's privacy."

"So, you're a fake Adam?"

"Adam runs on shifts. There is no real Adam."

"This must mean I win by default," Chris said.

So as not to be drowned out by the roar of applause and whistles, Chris shouted his claim to victory, his eyes darting around to the corners of the stage not shown on-screen. Following the staff's instructions, a waiter brought a silver cart from the kitchen. A perfectly white pie was placed in front of Chris.

"Just one?" X asked, leaning on the chair where Ibuki was sitting.

"So, which of us are you going to pie?" Ibuki asked as he squatted down in front of the cart and challenged Chris with his stare.

"Verbal aggression or lies," X said, "which do you hate more?"

Chris didn't respond. He took a deep breath as though trying to ease a burning in his chest.

"Time's up. We'll decide."

Ibuki shoved his whole face straight into the pie. The audience went wild. Ibuki shook his head from side to

JOSE ANDO

side like he was rubbing his face against the fur of a dog, breaking apart the soft surface of the pie. X stuck out his tongue and licked the cream off Ibuki's chin, exposing a single streak of cocoa-colored skin. Four eyes and two fake smiles that looked like they belonged in a shaving cream ad menaced the camera.

JACKSON WATCHED THE whole episode, and like the rest of the audience, he was shocked and moved. He cheered silently as they brought switching places to its ultimate form, but now that they'd exposed their secret, they couldn't use the trick anymore. Or rather, he saw no point in using it anymore. Jackson found it bittersweet.

6.

A club on a harbor in the suburbs was closing down for good. Its final gay night was Saturday.

Jerin's performing. Wanna go?

Jackson reached out to the others for the first time in forever. X declined, saying it was too much hassle. Ibuki already had plans to go. In the end, Jackson headed there alone.

He felt a presence behind him as he was typing a message and turned off his phone screen. The Athletius food court was starting to fill up, but the seats on either side of Jackson were still empty.

When he turned around, two other staff members were standing over him, debating whether to talk to him. Jackson moved over to one of the empty seats to let them sit.

After the pair next to him had been eating for a while, their conversation fizzled out and one of them struck up a conversation with Jackson.

JOSE ANDO

"Are you friends with Adam?"

Of course I am, he thought while letting out an internal sigh. "No, never met him," he said. Jackson opened his mouth wide and showed his teeth. Since X and Ibuki's episode had aired, the looks from strangers, which Jackson had forgotten, had made a return. He sensed he was smiling kind of like X did. The more he was alone, the more he started to copy the behavior of the other three. It was a sign that he needed time together with all four of them again.

Jackson arrived at the club on the last train, sometime past midnight, and showed the ticket QR code to get in. A paper band was wrapped around his wrist.

"I saw *Lies and Pies*."

The cautious comment came from a boy Jackson didn't know, who took a couple steps back and stared at Jackson embarrassedly. Caught off guard, Jackson failed to tell the guy he had the wrong person. He just said, "Oh yeah?" and feigned a similar embarrassment. The guy stood there like he wanted to say something else, or like he was waiting for Jackson to say something else, and didn't leave. Just as Jackson felt an unpleasant sweat coming on, someone grabbed his shoulder.

JACKSON ALONE

"Thank you!" the voice behind him said. "I'll let the real Adam know."

It was Ibuki. He'd arrived a little earlier and found Jackson by the bar, offering him a convenient escape.

"The reaction's been nuts, right?" Jackson said.

"The same thing just happened to me. People usually greet me as Ibuki, but today more people are mistaking me for X. And there are people who treat us like a duo now." Ibuki got a little worked up as he wove through the spaces between people.

"X isn't bummed about losing, is he?"

"Not at all. He may have lost on a technicality and gotten disqualified, but he still got a pretty sweet deal out of it."

"That's good. I wish he'd made it out tonight, though."

Jackson ordered two mojitos and passed one to Ibuki, who took cookies out of his pocket and handed one to Jackson. "I gotta catch up with my other friends. I'll see you later," he said, and vanished. Jackson was a bit disoriented for a moment, but ultimately, with nothing else to do, he stared down over the railing of the second-floor balcony at the ground floor.

When he unlocked his phone, the QR code he'd

used to get in was still on the screen. Why is it that the squares in the bottom-right corners of QR codes are smaller than in the other corners? Jackson wondered as he bit into the cookie. For some reason, he felt that the bottom-right corner looked like its growth had been stunted. The other three kept getting bigger and bigger and expanding their territories, but the bottom right stopped itself there and looked as though it had begun to get swallowed up by the haphazard pattern.

As he started to empathize with that square, a man next to him came up and cheersed him.

"A world-renowned club's final gay night!" the man said. "That in and of itself is art. But still. Basically at any club anywhere else in the world, when it's late enough and the house music comes on like this, a bunch of freaks rush to the front and start dancing like mad. But here? Nobody's doing that. Isn't it strange? Japanese people really just don't show their true selves, I think. They're just pretending to dance. Even with music this cool, almost no one responds to it. You know, this music, even this inorganic-sounding house music, has Black DNA flowing through it. This music comes from the Black people brought to America, you know. Back

JACKSON ALONE

then, they sealed up their own beats and made loops. Since they couldn't walk around town freely, they walked in circles to these restricted measures instead. That's the loop. The backbone of this track is samba. House music originated in Black culture, disco originated in Black culture, techno originated in Black culture, hip-hop originated in Black culture, soul and funk both originated in Black culture, rock originated in Black culture, jazz originated in Black culture, dubstep originated in Black culture, trap, too, originated in Black culture."

Jackson felt as though this man were pressuring him, telling him he'd better dance, and as he nodded along to what the man was saying, he started moving to the beat.

Though the surface of his body felt numb, he was awake in his core, and his thoughts were racing. Jackson wasn't all that into music, but the man's words spread through him like poison. His hair was done in a 70/30 part. He was Japanese and had studied abroad in England. Jackson wondered if this man would set him free or create a new imprisonment for him. The man said, "You've got *two* cultures." The first thing Jackson thought of when the man mentioned culture was Hotel Sagitari. I want to sleep in that room again, he thought.

JOSE ANDO

At one on the dot, the music stopped and a quiet sliced through the air like an enormous guillotine. The noise of those who had been partying this entire time reached Jackson's ears again. After a moment, drag queens took the stage to some Disney track. A prince and princess performed a sketch, then the curtain opened, and the show began. *They're just pretending to dance.* Jackson was disillusioned by everything he saw as he looked out from the second floor. They all looked like replicas. There were more people down there now, packed tight and responding to the queens' voguing with predetermined hand movements. In between acts came a parody of a famous drag number, and the onlookers who recognized it laughed like it was a competition to see who really got it. *Nothing is fun about this,* Jackson thought. He couldn't tell what was supposed to be fun about it. Jerin took the stage to a Beyoncé song. He wasn't wearing a straw hat or braids but a golden wave, a high-cut leotard, and stilettos. *I'm one of them,* Jackson thought to himself. *Me with my name-brand parka. X is one of them, too, with his black vintage clothes, his Ralph Lauren. Even Ibuki. He's made so much money, but he's still just one of them.* Everyone was basically facing the same direction, copying everyone else like it was a competition. If not, they were very intently stealing the moves of a bygone era and pretending to dance. He felt terrible. He started to feel sick. His stomach was telling him it was just a matter of time before he puked.

IBUKI TOOK A lap around the floor, shaking hands with anyone who came up to him as he went. The bar, the food stalls outside, the poolside, then back to the bar again.

As he scanned the drink menu, a hand reached out and pointed at the bottles of mineral water behind the bar. Under the black light the arm was a beautiful purple, and Ibuki could see the man was Black or part Black. When the hand grabbed the water, Ibuki saw something on the underside of the wrist giving off a bluish-white color, like a very tiny crystal.

He caught sight of it for only a second, but Ibuki was sure something was implanted there. He followed the man with his eyes as he was sucked back into the waves of people and then disappeared in the direction of the emergency exit.

JOSE ANDO

Next to that exit was a stairway. A narrow and rickety stairway that stretched up the wall like a vine. The top of it was enveloped in darkness so Ibuki couldn't see where it led, but the steps were so steep that they looked like they'd hit the ceiling if they continued much farther.

He approached the stairs and planted his foot on the first step. The pitch-black handrail felt rough, as though each time it'd been painted it was left to rust and then painted over again. With each step he took, the stairs creaked. At the first landing was a man crouched down and slumped over. Ibuki carefully stepped over him to make sure he didn't startle him into an outburst. As he continued ascending the stairs, it grew darker, and only the bass of the music below stayed pounding in his ears, as if all the other noises of the club were being filtered out. When he reached the top, there was a short catwalk and surprisingly, a small room. He'd been to this club countless times, but it was his first time up here. A security guard was sitting by the door, playing with his phone. Sensing Ibuki, he stood up. Ibuki shrank back in fear, but the guard stood there and said nothing.

Then, as though gesturing for him to enter, the guard

JACKSON ALONE

turned his body to the side to make space for Ibuki to pass. He pressed a card to the automatic door to open it for him.

Ibuki had imagined a standard VIP room, and his heart shrank at the absolute stillness of all the men gathered in there. Ibuki wandered in, pretending to be drunk, but his movements, and the little sounds that accompanied them, stood out dramatically. He rushed to stiffen his body.

In the next instant, everyone was looking in Ibuki's direction, and suddenly they applauded as if to congratulate him on having finally made it.

At a glance, there were at least twenty people there. They were almost all sitting, and those who were standing were leaning against the walls. It looked like a Pokémon GO hot spot, as all anyone was doing was staring at their phones. They were completely transfixed by their screens, no one was communicating with anybody else, but still they somehow formed a rough circle, in the middle of which were a few guys holding laptops.

Sweats, paint-splattered denim, chunky knits, satin trunks, slippers, sneakers, boots, bare skin, blankets, varsity jackets draped over shoulders, stoles with ethnic patterns, work jumpsuits: They were all dressed differently, however they wanted, and they were all mixed-raced Black boys. There was even one kid, who looked incredibly young, wearing a *gakuran*.

The celebratory greeting of these dark-skinned boys was so heartwarming that Ibuki fantasized for a second that he'd been invited. But from the moment he'd walked through the door, he'd known he couldn't let his guard down. The source of his anxiety was the strange man standing in the middle of the circle.

He was wearing a black turtleneck and a gold necklace under a purple suit. He looked like a Black man from the eighties varnished and made into a figurine, and he must've been at least thirty years older than the other boys there. His skin was black, but its blackness was different from that of the others around him. It was an unnatural blackness that looked as though it'd been painted on, and there was something unnervingly discordant about him, as though what covered him on the outside was different from who he was on the inside. After observing him carefully, Ibuki realized that he alone was a Japanese man dressed like a Black man.

JACKSON ALONE

"Did you have a hard time finding the place?" the man asked in his raspy voice.

"Not really."

"I guess you wouldn't."

The man took the laptop from the boy in sweats and turned it to Ibuki.

The grainy security footage showed Ibuki a few minutes ago staring at the stairs, his face enclosed in a fluorescent square.

"It's only been a little over an hour since you got to the club. I wonder if it was really an accident that you made it to this room."

"You've been monitoring me?"

"Today's the first time we've been following you this carefully. But your movements have been so conspicuous that you've been easy to track."

Ibuki laughed to disguise what he really felt.

"How'd you all come up with that idea of trading places?" the man continued. "It was fascinating to watch. Of course, with a little facial recognition, it's easy to keep you all sorted. But to the naked eye, you all really do look similar. My staff got confused every time."

JOSE ANDO

At the word *staff*, Ibuki took another look at the boys around him.

"Not *slaves*?" he said.

The man didn't answer the question and instead gave a wry laugh. Judging from the atmosphere of the room, this man was their boss.

"Really, without one of these you shouldn't be able to get in here," the boss said, now taking the hand of the boy in sweats and shining a penlight on it. In his wrist was the same thing Ibuki had seen at the bar: a square implanted there, shining bluish white.

"What is that? A chip?" Ibuki asked, narrowing his eyes.

"Something like that."

"You put one of those in all of them."

"That's right. They're a team, after all."

"So you branded them like cattle."

"Oh, don't make it sound so bad. We anesthetize them and then just shoot it in. It takes a second. And it holds far more information than the QR code on your shirts."

"So you're the one who sent those shirts to Jackson and the others."

JACKSON ALONE

"Not me," the man said. "Us."

"What was this to you? You, plural."

"We intended it as part of our recruitment efforts."

"To this place?"

"Yes. Oh, I haven't introduced myself yet," the man said. "My name is Murphy."

"Even though you're Japanese?"

"I'm Masahito. People call me Murphy."

"Yuck."

Someone clicked his tongue, and the sticky sound of saliva filled the room. One of the two boys in the corner sharing a blanket stood up and rushed past Ibuki.

Ibuki felt the vibrations of the boy's footsteps grow weaker as he listened to him make his way down the stairs to the club.

"Is there trouble?" Murphy asked the boy who remained wrapped in the blanket. The boy gave an obligatory smile and nodded silently.

"Data about Black people fetches a good price, you know."

"Just like porn." Ibuki laughed.

"Much better than porn. Crime data."

"Who do you sell it to?"

"The police, of course."

"And what do they get out of buying that kind of thing?"

"They monitor criminal activity and all that."

"To make arrests?"

"I guess you could say their goal is to be ready to arrest anyone at any time. Their goal is the monitoring itself. I don't ask how our customers use the data we sell, and I don't much care, but the one thing I can say is that they don't care about you all as individuals. They're happy to collect data about anyone as long as they fall into a category like yours. As long as they can use it to keep an eye on dangerous-looking people. Targets with unusual behavior patterns or unusual appearances. Black gays make the best bait for them, right?"

"Sounds like a conspiracy theory."

"It just looks that way because there are a bunch of Black boys gathered in an attic." Murphy laughed, expecting Ibuki to laugh along.

"But there's one fake mixed in with the rest," Ibuki said. "You've got this many people just to monitor us?"

"Ha ha, you aren't worth that much. Sorry. Since so many people were coming out tonight, we rounded up the team so we could gather data. We're probably the only ones here not drinking. Not that they're old enough anyway."

Most of the boys were unresponsive, but a few of them forced smiles.

"These three were in charge of tracking you."

Murphy waved his right hand and gestured toward the three boys closest to him.

"They ordered those shirts and had them delivered, too," Murphy said.

The boy in a jumpsuit said, "Hey," and the other two only smiled. Ibuki sensed no agency in their reactions, just like all the other boys. They all sat there like plants sapped of their nourishment, quietly collecting data.

"I have so many questions!" Ibuki said. "Why make sure all your staff members are Black mixed kids? Is this some fetish of yours?"

"Oh, it's not just a fetish. How about this. Why don't we test out my special talent?" Murphy sat back down in his chair.

"Ibuki," he said, "where were you born?"

"Fussa."

"What year?"

JOSE ANDO

"1992."

"So your dad is Yulian and your mom is Mika, right?"

He was right. "You figure that out from your monitoring?" Ibuki played it cool, but he had goose bumps.

"No, we don't have data for anything that far back. This is just from memory. I remember everything from back in the day—where the friends I hung out with lived, who had kids when. All the things you see here are the fruits of a good memory and a network. I even remember phone numbers from back then."

To take further control of the conversation, Murphy locked his eyes on Ibuki. "Before you were born," he continued, "near a harbor similar to this one but some distance from here, there was an even bigger club. I used to hang out with them there all the time. Mika was a good kid, but Yulian was a piece of shit. He'd always get into fights. Eventually Mika got pregnant, but her body was worn-down from all the drugs, and she had a miscarriage. She stopped coming to the club after that, but Yulian would still show up from time to time. And then, a few years later, you were born."

"And then a few decades later, you were left all alone," Ibuki said, "clinging to those good ol' days?"

JACKSON ALONE

"You know, I think we're similar. I think you'll meet a similar fate. I've got one piece of advice for you," he said. "Do you know what a washed-up old man who stops getting invited to parties should do to make sure he doesn't get lonely?"

"Hell if I know." There was amusement in Ibuki's eyes, amusement directed at something truly pathetic.

"You must *expand!*" Murphy said. "First clothes, money. Then new locations, and the people who come there, you must absorb them all."

The image on the security monitor changed at regular intervals, and each time it did, certain faces in the crowd were detected and marked with fluorescent squares.

"Kind of reminds me of an airport," Ibuki said.

"It's oddly calming to watch, isn't it?"

"I dunno, I'm kind of over it. I think I'll see myself out now."

"You're not good at being angry."

"I'm not actually angry. I just find your voice unpleasant."

"'Cause it's hoarse from too much drinking? I like it. I thought it sounded kind of Black."

"That word." Ibuki rubbed his temple with his right

hand like he was suffering from a migraine. "Do you want to know how the word *Black* sounds to us when someone who's not Black says it?"

"Ooh, do tell."

"It's kind of like . . . It's really *guttural*. It really grates our ears."

Ibuki turned toward the exit.

"About the advice I just gave you," Murphy said. "You have another option: Be absorbed."

"You're inviting me to join you?"

"I can make it worth your while."

"And if I say no?"

"Well, you lot are my favorites, so I'm not going to sell you out too soon. I'll just keep watching."

"And if I join, you'll stop monitoring the others?"

"Sure, no problem."

"Old man, you sure accepted that fast."

Ibuki walked back toward Murphy. He stepped onto the carpet, still wearing his shoes, and over the legs of the boys all around him. Murphy extended his right hand to shake on it. As Ibuki approached with his eyes turned elsewhere, he reached out and gripped Murphy's right hand with his left hand twisted upside down, then shoved his own right hand into Murphy's turtlenecked solar plexus. His hand slipped on the sweat, lost its grip on the churrasco knife, and for a second, the knife's handle was swallowed up by the air. It took only that instant for the knife to go cold, and when Ibuki gripped it again, the chill of it sent a shiver down his spine. He pulled it as far to the side as he could before ripping it out, and he felt the sensation of something incredibly hard breaking as the contents of Murphy's sweater poured out. Solid masses of glittering silver scattered across the floor. They shone like drops of water as they bounced and tumbled. What came flowing out of him was not blood but a stream of coins.

"E, pronto!" Murphy shouted, clapping his hands together. And then the boys, who, until that moment, had looked so bored, screamed for joy like children and descended on Murphy all at once. Using their arms and the clothes they were wearing, they began to scrape up the coins spilling out of him.

"*Oww!*" Murphy screamed, and all the boys around him stepped back.

Ibuki thought he saw Murphy's right ear wriggle

slowly like the suction cup of an octopus. Suddenly blood came pouring out from where his ear met his head. One of the boys screamed, and that set everyone off running in different directions.

"*Oww!*" Murphy screamed again. No one was touching him, but now his nose was twisted unnaturally as though being squished back into his skull. It was as if he were being toyed with by some sort of ghost—his nose slowly caved in and downward before suddenly being yanked up. And then blood started to spill from there as well.

It was wires. Wires so thin you couldn't see them from a distance, but they were tied to Murphy's face.

All the boys started shouting now. *He's caught on something. What? It's like strings or something. From where? Behind. It's not me, look! I'm not holding anything. Wait, they're coming this way, too.*

There, among the mass of shouting boys all desperate for the truth, were voices of urgency, and voices of indifference, and voices of clear enjoyment: Everyone circled Murphy, confused, and before they knew it, the wires were pulling his chin up.

Don't move.

JACKSON ALONE

Someone pushed someone else, and the crowd shifted around them.

In that moment, the wires seemed to loosen their grip on Murphy's mouth, then, just as the mass started moving again, they dug straight into his neck.

There was the click of someone flipping off a switch, and red shadow cloaked the room, erasing all its colors. Then came the sounds of light bulbs shattering, and everything went dark.

The boys surrounding Murphy stumbled about with all their might, and the vibrations of their movements traveled to Ibuki's feet. Confusion pervaded the room.

What's going on? I have no idea. Who's doing this? What the fuck. Serves him right. Now we can say whatever we want. Can anyone see anything? Yeah, no. Hey, is he dead? He's bloody. Fucking gross. Hey, they were wrapped around his neck a second ago, right? Those string things. You mean his throat's been slit? That's fucking awful. Does that mean someone here did it? Yeah, so that means now's our only chance. Who did it? We can worry about that later. He's still alive. Someone, help me. Hurry.

At that call for help, Ibuki heard footsteps making their way to the center of the room. His hand on the door, Ibuki stood there frightened till it was all over. The vibrations of Murphy stomping on the ground vanished. The stink of shit filled the room. After a while, someone's phone shined a pure white light on Murphy's face. His eyes were open wide, as though he were staring into the light. A voice sounded out: *It's over.*

What do we do? On the count of three, we all run, right? What's the point? We're all gonna get caught anyway. Okay, so, the story is someone, one person, went crazy and the rest of us know nothing. Now we can run, right? The story? That's the truth, isn't it? There's no way just one person could've pulled that off by themselves, though. What do you mean? Never mind. I mean, aren't there cameras in this room, too? Yeah, that's why we killed him with wires, so no one could see on the camera. So does that mean someone here is going to get caught? Probably, but the chances are like twenty-something to one. And outside of here there's definitely more people. More who look like us. We all wanted to kill him, so it's better this way. Better than one of us doing it alone. Yeah. You're right. I guess that's true. From here on out it's Russian roulette, so look out for yourselves. Let's avoid each other for a while. See you again somewhere. Today

JACKSON ALONE

was fun. Stay safe. Forever and ever. Okay, let's go. One. Two. Three!

Shouting, the boys flooded out of the room. They shook off the security guard and, screaming and crying, descended the stairs single file. They were raving mad and all dressed differently, their individual styles odd assortments, yet they walked in lockstep. Ibuki bounded desperately down the stairs in the middle of their line. All these Black boys in gaudy clothes made it to the dance floor and dissolved into the colorful crowd.

Come to think of it, what was Ibuki even wearing? He examined his own body. He had on a shirt he didn't recognize on top of his own clothes. Did that mean he was in disguise? Could he make a run for it like that? His anxiety refused to fade. Murphy's words lingered in his mind: *With a little facial recognition, it's easy to keep you all sorted.*

All that remained in the attic was Murphy's corpse, but outside, the club was still packed. Screams of terror and exhilaration melted together until they were impossible to differentiate, and for a moment it seemed this was any ordinary club.

Some of the boys who'd fled ran straight off the club

premises. Others hid in areas labeled DO NOT ENTER and then snuck off along the bank of the harbor, startled along the way by men pissing into the ocean. Others stayed put—danced as though absolutely nothing had just happened, or got in line for drinks.

After he puked in the bathroom, Jackson returned to the dance floor and got the feeling that the number of men who looked like him had increased while he was gone. He made eye contact with a group of four hanging out by the stairwell. Their skin was also cocoa-colored, but they didn't look like him. They were not Jerin, or Ibuki, or X, but men he'd never seen before.

"That was wild, right?" said one of them, revealing a silver tooth.

"Yeah, it was bad."

"Did you just puke?" one said to Jackson.

"Yeah."

"But good thing you got out of there. For real."

He accepted a bottle of water from one of them and drank. The surface of his body still felt numb, but his core was wide awake and finally warmed up, and he felt things were going to get better.

"Was there a fight?" Jackson asked.

JACKSON ALONE

"Huh?" The four froze for a second at Jackson's question.

"Look, look at all the police!" Jackson said.

"Forget you saw anything," one of them said as they all turned away. Then they vanished toward the exit as though they'd just remembered they had somewhere to be.

Murphy's body was carried down the stairs. There was a brief commotion, and the men trained their cameras on the scene, traded information and conspiracies, or left the club before getting dragged into any trouble. But the commotion didn't last long. Most of the men went back to enjoying themselves. There was still time left for their desperate partying.